CANDY KISSES

•

Jean C. Gordon

The characters and events portrayed in this book are fictitious. Any similarity to real persons, living or dead, is coincidental and not intended by the author.

Printed in the United States of America.

Published by Montlake Romance
P.O. Box 400818
Las Vegas, NV 89140

ISBN-13: 9781477813485
ISBN-10: 1477813489

This title was previously published by Avalon Books; this version has been reproduced from the Avalon book archive files.

Thanks to Bonnie, Chris, Colleen, Roxane, and
Thomasine for seeing me through to the end.

Chapter One

Call Stacie.

Candace "Candy"—she'd never forgive her parents for that one—Price stared at the bold scrawl for a split second before ripping the sticky note from the hall mirror and crumpling it into the wastebasket.

Jeez! The woman had being a pain in the ass down to a fine art.

It couldn't be more than twenty minutes since she'd left headquarters. What could Stacie possibly want from her now? Probably to rush back and make the nine hundredth revision to the two-paragraph press release she'd left on Stacie's desk on her way out, about New York gubernatorial candidate Dan Burling's appearance at the state fair.

Candy picked up the stack of mail from the hall table

and shuffled through it as she walked into the living room. The very quiet living room. In fact, the big old brownstone reeked of quiet, not like when she used to stop by to see Mara, when Ali, Ben, and Jesse all still lived here.

She sat in the overstuffed recliner and wondered who would be moving into the other rooms in the fall. Probably no one she knew. All her grad school friends—it seemed—had left for jobs in other places.

"Hey, you're home early." Mike Wheeler, her sometimes landlord and sole roommate for the summer—unless you counted Sheba, the twenty-pound Persian cat—stood in the doorway.

"Yeah, it's only six forty, a new record. Don't tell me. You've been home since four, been to the Y, and stopped in for a cold beer at Sutters."

Mike leaned against the doorjamb and gazed down at her, eyes twinkling. "You know how it is when you choose to have a 'no-brainer' job that's 'way below your abilities' and doesn't 'stimulate any ambition.' You can be done with work and ready to play by two, no sweat."

Candy stopped tossing the unwanted mail on the coffee table. "Mara told you I said that?"

Mike gave her wicked smile. "Did you see my note that Stacie called?"

Candy shot for a totally blank expression. "Note? I didn't see any note. If I didn't see a note, I wouldn't know that Stacie called. And I wouldn't call her back to learn there's something I have to do for her at home tonight because it absolutely can't wait until tomorrow, even though it probably doesn't need to be done at all."

Mike's smile widened to a grin that creased the corners of his mouth almost into dimples and caused a little flutter in her stomach. His ex-girlfriend must be kicking herself for letting him go. Except for that low-ambition thing.

"There was no call. There was no note on the mirror," Mike deadpanned. Then he grew serious. "It's time you chilled about work. You don't have to be at Stacie's beck and call. The job will still be there tomorrow."

Candy nodded in agreement, then bit her lip. "Maybe I should call Stacie. It could be important."

Mike shook his head as if she were hopeless.

"It could be. Every so often Stacie freaks about something real." She checked her watch. "I hope there's no problem with Dan's town hall meeting in Saratoga." Candy ran through a mental checklist of all the preparations she'd made and any potential glitches she might have overlooked and came up blank. Everything should be covered.

She looked back up at Mike. His mouth was still drawn down in disapproval. So what if she gave one hundred and ten percent to her job, which she knew only made Stacie expect more? She wanted to make the most of her time in Albany so she could move on to a real career in a real city.

"At least finish looking at your mail first," Mike said,

clearly giving up. He started toward his room off the dining room, stopped in front of her chair, and stooped to pick up a letter on the floor.

He looked at the envelope and laughed. "Albany Law School. Are your brothers having their friends formally petition you for dates now?"

"Give me that." She grabbed the letter and ripped it open. She scanned it quickly. "If you must know. It's a response to my application."

"For a job? I thought, despite your spawn-of-Satan boss, you liked your job."

"I do. Most of the time. I, um, applied to law school."

"Law school? As in another associate for Price, Price & Price, LLC?"

"No, I wouldn't practice with my brothers. I haven't actually decided to go to law school. It's kind of a bet." She rubbed her temples. Mara must not have told him everything, or he'd know about the bet.

"A bet?"

"Yes." She sighed. "A bet. I made the mistake of pointing out what a jerk one of the blind dates Alex set me up with was. That if he could get through law school, anyone could."

"I see." Mike lounged back on the couch and clasped his hands behind his head, obviously ready for all the gory details.

"Do you?" He couldn't. Not really. Sometimes, even she didn't understand the dynamics between her and her older brothers. Even though she knew they loved her just as she was, she always felt she had to prove something to them.

"Let me guess. They all know the guy and defended him."

"Something like that."

"And," Mike continued, "one of them challenged you to get into law school. So you did."

He was good, unless . . . "Mara told you, didn't she?"

"Not exactly. But she did tell me about some of the blind dates your brothers set up. I got the idea."

Candy felt a blush creeping up her neck. It wasn't like she needed her brothers to get her dates. They just did, and it humored her father that she was going out with "nice" men. She refolded the letter, creasing each bend. What did she care what Mike might think? They were just roommates. Besides, Mara surely had told her more things about Mike than Mara had told Mike about her.

"So, did you get accepted?"

She put the letter back in the envelope. "No, this just confirms that they're considering my application."

"You know you could be bumping someone who really wants to go to law school, just to prove a point with your brothers." Every well-toned inch of Mike radiated disgust.

He didn't have to get huffy. "I wasn't being malicious," she defended herself. "Law school might be a good move. I've had the idea in the back of my mind for a while. It could help my political career."

Mike's eyes narrowed.

"What? Working with Dan's campaign has got me thinking that maybe politics is the way to make a difference." There, that should bring his boil back to a simmer. Mike was a do-gooder. Not that it mattered whether he thought she was flighty and self-centered.

"Hmmm, from what I heard, you took the job just to have a job. So you wouldn't have to go back home."

Mara again. She'd have to have a long talk with that girl. "I might have started out like that, but politics could be my niche. I can help people without having to live from paycheck to paycheck like Jesse."

Mike arched an eyebrow in question.

"Do you know what he earns?"

The eyebrow remained arched.

"He has a master's in social work."

"I have a good idea," Mike answered dryly.

She sank a bit in the sofa. Mike's job as property manager of an alliance to provide housing to disabled vets probably didn't pay any more than that of a social worker.

"And, unless there's something I don't know, you're not exactly pulling in the big bucks. Or were you BS-ing me when you said you couldn't afford to pay a full half share of the housing expenses for the summer?"

She sank even lower. "I can't," she admitted. "Besides, you said that you and your father had retainers from the students who are moving into the other rooms for the second summer session and in the fall, so I didn't have to pay more."

Candy scooted back up in the chair. "And my work has potential. It's a stepping stone to bigger things."

Mike gave her a patronizing smile.

But her work *was* important. Dan Burling was promising to make all kinds of positive reforms if he was elected, and she could move into the governor's media corps. Then, who knew? Maybe Washington. Of course, she might have to take that detour through law school, but she'd think about that when it happened.

She gathered the rest of her mail and stood. "I think I'll go upstairs and check my e-mail." Like she had to report to Mike where she was going and what she was doing. Jeez, he wasn't one of her brothers and she wasn't fifteen anymore.

"Tell Mara I said hi."

"I will." Candy smiled to herself. Maybe she should help Mike find some women to date. To help him forget that his old girlfriend dumped him. Could be fun. She crossed the room and started up the stairs.

"Candy?"

She looked over the railing at Mike. He didn't want to talk about her, did he? Not that she wouldn't like to. She was a sucker for love stories—good *or* bad—if it would help Mike, but Candy was beat tonight. "Yeah?" she answered.

"Raoule made ravioli for the guys at the vet house

tonight. If you're hungry, there's a container in the refrigerator."

Candy gauged the effort that would be required to get ravioli against her hunger. "Thanks, but I'll just have an energy bar while I'm checking my e-mail." She turned and climbed the rest of the stairs. Pausing at the top, she glanced back to find Mike still standing by the sofa watching her. Weird. Had he wanted her to eat dinner with him? Maybe he did want to talk. Maybe he was lonely. She would hang out with him—soon—she promised herself.

Once Candy was out of sight, Mike grinned. She was a piece of work. And a nicely put-together one at that. He'd thoroughly enjoyed the way her pencil skirt delineated her behind as she climbed the stairs. He whistled off to the kitchen to have some of Raoule's ravioli.

Beep, beep, beep, came the familiar sound of the instant-message window opening.

Priceless: <Mara! I know you're there, hiding behind that away message.>

Candy typed frenetically into the window, hit the enter key, and sat back to wait for Mara's answer.

She blew an errant wisp of hair off her forehead. She really needed a haircut but was almost too embarrassed to call her stylist since she'd missed the last two appointments she'd scheduled. Maybe early Saturday morning. She fingered the ends of her hair. She could use some highlights, too. Who was she kidding? Whenever she scheduled the appointment, Stacie would somehow know and need her desperately for some work emergency—right then.

What Albany really needed was a twenty-four-hour salon. Maybe she should run some numbers on it. See if it would fly. Hair styling wasn't anything she'd considered before. It probably was more interesting than law, corporate law for sure. She could franchise. No more Stacie.

"Hey Girl." The robotlike computer voice called to Candy, letting her know that Mara had turned off her away message and was back online.

MaraNara: <What's up?>
Priceless: <About time. I'd almost embarked on a whole new career while I was waiting for you.>
MaraNara: <Not again!>
Priceless: <Never mind that. Did you repeat everything I ever told you to Mike?>
MaraNara: <Mike?>
Priceless: <Yes, Mike. You might remember him. Tall, dark wavy hair, just a hint of dimples when he smiles. The guy you've known since preschool, your other "best friend.">

MaraNara: <That Mike.☺ Sure, I might have told him things you said.>

Priceless: <Like he has no ambition. I never said that.>

MaraNara: <No, but you did say that he could do better for himself.>

Priceless: <I meant that in a good way. I don't think he took it that way.>

MaraNara: <And that matters?>

Priceless: <No, yes. He's the only person left here to talk with.>

MaraNara: <So you and Mike have been talking?>

Priceless: <I think I said that. ☺>

MaraNara: <He's a good listener, among other things.>

Priceless: <Yeah? Then why didn't you guys ever get together?>

MaraNara: <No mystique.>

Priceless: <??>

MaraNara: <We've been over this before. I've known him since I was three. Longer than I've known you. He's like family.>

Priceless: <Say no more.>

MaraNara: <But better than my family. Besides, I was with his friend Jesse.>

Priceless: <Yeah, like forever. I was sure he'd go down to Asheville with you.>

MaraNara: <Better he didn't.>

Priceless: <Well, he was unreasonable. He really couldn't expect you to give up the opportunity to be the activity director of a resort as large as Glenhaven to stick around *Small*-bany to do what? Hostess at the Turf Inn?>

A pop-up ad for "the lowest mortgage rate on the web" blocked the instant message window. Candy clicked it closed and waited and waited for Mara's reply.

Priceless: <You still there?>

MaraNara: <Yep. How's your dad?>

Priceless: <Doing better, he says. But open heart surgery is not little thing.>

MaraNara: <Better enough that you'd feel okay coming down here in the fall?>

Priceless: <I can't get any time off before the primary. With b-on-wheels Stacie, who knows if I can ever get any time off.>

MaraNara: <No, I meant move down. The assistant to the PR director is leaving in September.>

Priceless: <Don't tempt me. I've got to stick this job out until the election. I'd never hear the end of it from Price, Price & Price, LLC if I don't.>

MaraNara: <You have got to get out from under the thumbs of those brothers of yours. It's archaic.>

Priceless: <They mean well. They think they're

taking care of me. Besides, if Dan wins, I could have a place in the governor's media office.>
MaraNara: <And if you came down here, you'd still be writing press releases and the scenery is a lot better. A constant parade of hotties. The conventions here are not your usual middle-aged businessmen.>

Candy hesitated. She must be tired. This was an opportunity to get out of *Small*-bany, and she felt no compulsion to jump right on it.

Priceless: <I'll think about it.>
MaraNara: <Do! Don't be like Jesse and blow an opportunity like this. Things are really hot down here.>
Priceless: <Speaking of hot, I was thinking I might try fixing Mike up. What do you think?>
MaraNara: <Why would you think he needs fixing up?>
Priceless: <Well, it's been a while since he's been with anyone but she who will not be named. He seems a little lost.>
MaraNara: <Lost? That doesn't sound like him. He always knows exactly where he's going, what he's doing.>
Priceless: <That's a good thing.>
MaraNara: <Not always.>
Priceless: <So, I should back off?>

MaraNara: <Go for it. You need something for entertainment other than work. And since you seem to limit your own dating to blind dates your brothers set up for you . . . >
Priceless: <Not true!>
MaraNara: <True!>
Priceless: <I'm just really busy.>
MaraNara: <Stacie is still working you to death?>
Priceless: <I blew her off tonight. Didn't return her after-hours phone call.>
MaraNara: <Good for you. My phone's ringing.>

Candy took an energy bar from her stash in the desk drawer and ripped it open and took a big bite. Maybe Mara was right about her social life. She couldn't remember the last time she made a date of her own. She never went anywhere anymore where there was anyone to ask her out.

MaraNara: <Hey, do you mind? It's one of those hotties I mentioned. So, I'm going to sign off. Okay? Bye.>

Guess that was that. Candy checked her Buddy List to see if anyone else was online. Not that she felt like talking anymore. She looked at the clock. Ten twenty-two. This was sad. She was so beat, she might as well go to bed. Her stomach growled. There *was* Raoule's ravioli. She clicked Shut Down and turned the computer off. But the ravioli was all the way downstairs. Downstairs and at the other side of the house in the kitchen. Her bed was right here, soft and inviting. The bed won out. *Pathetic*, she thought as she drifted off to sleep.

Chapter Two

With stealth that would have made a special forces commander proud, Candy opened her desk drawer and pulled out her purse. She slid the mud-red vinyl chair away from the steel-gray desk just far enough to slip out. The chair creaked and she glanced around. The coast looked clear. No sign of Stacie.

Candy took one step toward the door, then another, past the volunteers who were busy stapling VOTE FOR BURLING signs to paint-stirrer handles. Ten more steps, a push of the glass door, and she'd be outside, free to enjoy a sandwich at the deli down the street.

"Candy!" Stacie's voice grated like fingernails on a chalkboard. "Are you going out for lunch?"

"Erm, yeah. It's almost two o'clock."

"Great!"

Not for her, Candy was sure.

"I need someone to run these signs down to the campus office," Stacie said. "Those punk kids stole every Burling sign in the campus area—again."

Candy looked pointedly at the sign makers. "Couldn't one of the volunteers take them over, maybe on their way home?" At least one of them had to be a student.

"Can't wait. Besides, they're all busy."

Like she wasn't? "What about that mailing list I'm converting from Excel to Access? I was just going to grab a sandwich and get right back on it." That is, after a leisurely walk to the deli, some down time to eat a sandwich, and a leisurely walk back.

"Scrap that."

Candy's heart sank. "But I've spent all morning on it. You need it to get those announcements out about Dan's western New York appearances. You know, make sure the voters out there know that just because Dan is from downstate doesn't mean he doesn't care about upstate too."

Stacie waved her off. "No, we'll send the announcements out. I was talking with Todd this morning about those extra computer connections I want, and he said we can do the mail merge right from Excel."

Candy looked at her watch. This morning? I was after two now. She bit her tongue until she felt she could speak in an inside voice, as Miss Patty at preschool used to say. "I told you yesterday that I could do the merge from Excel."

"You did?" Stacie looked at her as if she had just noticed her standing there. "I don't recall. But, we're wasting time. The signs are over there."

The effort to keep her mouth from dropping open made her jaw ache. Wasting time? And what had she been doing all day? The letters and envelopes could have been all printed and ready to be stuffed. She was beginning to think that this whole job was a waste of time—her time.

"Everyone," Stacie commanded, and the room hushed. "Candy is going out to the deli. If you want anything, just give her your order and money."

Candy's mouth did drop open at this announcement. She'd been promoted from Stacie's lackey to everyone's lackey. She was too old for this. She really would have to rethink why she'd thought this job had career potential. The volunteers started shouting orders, and she grabbed a pen and pad from her desk. If she had wanted to be a waitress, she could think of any number of restaurants that would pay more than she was earning here.

"What's all the excitement?" Everyone's attention turned to the man who had come through the front door.

"Dan, what a surprise," Stacie greeted him in a sugary voice she reserved for people other than her underlings. "We weren't expecting you until tomorrow."

Stacie sashayed across the room to take Dan's arm and lead him over to the table where the volunteers were assembling signs.

"I wanted to go over those western New York appearances with you," Dan said.

Candy watched with interest. Stacie's whole demeanor had softened. She had to admit that Stacie was a beautiful woman, although her sharp edge detracted from it. Her roan-brown hair fell smoothly to her shoulders, and she had one of those flawless figures that could wear anything to perfection.

Dan looked at the pile of signs. The ones Stacie wanted her to deliver. "Looks like you've all been busy."

"Yes, we're just now going to break for lunch," Stacie said. "Candy is running down to the deli."

"Do you want me to pick up something for you?" Candy asked. She held up her pad and pen.

Dan turned to her, and Stacie gave her a look that could reduce Mount Everest to ash. What was with that?

"No, thanks. I had lunch," Dan answered. He began shaking hands with the volunteers while she took their lunch orders.

Stacie's smile returned until Dan spent a little too long talking with a petite blond college student whose hiphugger jeans and crop-top showcased the emerald stud in her belly button.

Wow! That's it! Stacie had the hots for Dan. Who would have thought?

She gathered up the completed signs. "Stacie, I'll need your car to deliver these."

Stacie frowned.

"I am not taking the city bus." She stood her ground.

Stacie went to her office and returned with the keys. "You really should get a car of your own," she said.

Candy took the keys. On what she earned, she could afford a place of her own *or* a car. She'd opted for a place of her own over living up north at her dad's in Victory Hills, in the middle of nowhere.

"I'll be back," she called over her shoulder as she made her escape.

Candy watched the sandwiches pile up on the deli counter beside the drinks and soup. Stacie, of course, had had to order soup. She hadn't bothered taking the car to the deli since she could see every parking space on the block was taken. So she had gotten her leisurely stroll to the deli. And she was going to get a couple more to cart all the food back. She'd have to make at least two trips, one with the sandwiches and one with the drinks.

The door buzzed, signaling the arrival of another late lunch customer. She took the bags, turned, and almost ran into Mike.

"Hey," he said, his distracted expression changing to a smile.

"Hey, yourself. What are you doing downtown?"

"Had to check out a zoning law change at city hall."

"A problem?"

"Don't know yet. Hungry?" he asked, pointing at the multiple plastic bags.

"You won't believe it. Stacie sent me out to pick up lunch for everyone at headquarters. Then, I have to run election placards down to the campus."

"The drinks are all yours too?"

"Yep."

"Let me get my sandwich and I'll give you a hand. I ordered ahead."

The clerk handed Mike a wrapped package and added his drink to the collection. He paid for his order and picked up the drink trays. She pushed the door open with her shoulder and held it for Mike and the drinks.

"Thanks," he said.

"Thank you." She nodded at the trays he was juggling.

"No problem. My car is right across the street." They darted over between cars. He put the drinks on the floor in the back seat and reached for the sandwich bags. She pulled her sandwich out and handed them over. He stowed them too, and opened the passenger door for her.

"How does Stacie expect you to get the signs uptown?" he asked as he turned the ignition. "I can drive you."

She pulled Stacie's car keys from her bag and jingled them. "Bad precedent. If Stacie thinks I have access to transportation, she'll expect me to donate it to the cause. Much as I'd like the company"—and she would, she realized—"I'd better drive myself."

He pulled his Jetta into the small off-street parking area that came with headquarters' building rental, rolling to within inches of the back of Stacie's car.

She grabbed his knee, fearing he was going to dent Stacie's Z4.

Mike grinned at her as he turned the car off. "Scare you?"

She lifted her hand and returned it to her lap, heat and cold alternately flowing through her. "Not you. Stacie. I'd never hear the end of it if you put so much as a hairline scratch on her bumper. And I shudder to think what it would cost to replace a BMW bumper."

He laughed. "Can't wait to meet her in person."

They grabbed the food and headed in.

"About time." Stacie's screech greeted them.

Dan was obviously gone, returning Stacie to her usual self. Maybe there was some way they could get Dan to spend more time at headquarters? Better yet, send Stacie with Dan on his cross-state campaigning. From what Candy had seen earlier this afternoon, she doubted Stacie would mind. Of course, she would have to leave media headquarters under someone else's direction. As Stacie's first assistant, Candy was the logical choice. She was liking this idea better and better.

"Where do you want these?" Mike raised the drink trays to Candy.

Before she could answer, Stacie stepped over, a welcoming smile on her face. “Right here.” She took his elbow and guided him to the sign table in the back.

He looked down and smiled back, giving her a blatant once-over.

“Are you a friend of Candy’s?” Stacie asked in a voice almost as sweet as the one she’d used earlier with Dan.

Yes, Candy wanted to shout for some neurotic reason. *He’s my friend, not yours. Don’t touch.*

“Yes,” he answered. “I’m Mike Wheeler.”

“Stacie Martin.” She introduced herself.

Although she had dropped his elbow, Stacie stayed close by Mike’s side as the others clamored for their food.

Disappointment and irritation pricked Candy. Maybe Stacie didn’t have a thing for Dan after all. Maybe she turned all sweet around any attractive man who didn’t work for her. Worse, now that Mike had met Stacie and seen how beautiful she was, Candy would have a hard time calling her the wicked witch or spawn of Satan in front of him.

“Here are the sandwiches.” She plunked the bags on the table. “They’re all marked. And here’s the order and change.” She dropped the coins and bills on the table in front of Stacie, knowing that she would be compelled to sort it out. “I’ve got to run those signs uptown.”

“Wait up.” Mike caught her at the door.

So, he wasn’t caught hopelessly in Stacie’s allure,

whatever that might be. Not that it mattered, except that Mike was a nice guy and she would hate to see him in Stacie's clutches.

"You sure you don't want me to drive you to the campus?" He looked up at the clock on the bank down the street. "It's almost three thirty. We could head home after you drop off the signs. After that, Jesse and some others are getting together a soccer game at Richfield Park if you want to come with us."

She bit her bottom lip. Leaving early. Watching Mike in action. He'd probably wear those cutoffs that hung low on his hips and showed off his cute butt. It was tempting. Very tempting. But there was that mailing that had to be out.

"No, I've got to get a bunch of letters out for Stacie."

"That Stacie is something," he said.

"Yeah?"

"Like Dr. Jekyll and Mr. Hyde."

"You caught that, then?"

"Couldn't miss it."

She knew Mike was a good guy, that he'd see right through Stacie. Okay, so he had her going for a minute or two.

"Sure you can't make the game?" he cajoled. "We'll stop by the Lark Tavern for pizza afterward."

The eager, boyish grin that accompanied his invitation almost did her in. She was ready to chuck the signs, the letters, the job and call it a day—almost.

"Maybe I can catch part of the game," she said.

"Sure," he said.

"See you later." She climbed in Stacie's BMW and, as she backed out, caught Mike crossing the street in the rearview mirror. He did have a cute butt.

Candy changed into a T-shirt and pajama bottoms while she waited for her computer to boot. By the time she had gotten the letters out for Stacie, it was dusk and not worth changing and going over to Richfield Park.

Hey girl, the computer called. Mara was on.

MaraNara: <Wassup?>
Priceless: <Wait till I tell you.>
MaraNara: <Oooo, good stuff?>
Priceless: <Stacie has a thing for Dan.>
MaraNara: <No way.>
Priceless: <Way. I don't know why I didn't notice earlier.>
MaraNara: <Tell all.>
Priceless: <Dan stopped in at headquarters unexpectedly and she turned from the wicked witch of the west to all sweet and kittenish.>
MaraNara: <That's it?>
Priceless: <Maybe you had to be there. It was dramatic.>
MaraNara: <Keep me posted.>
Priceless: <What's up with you? Going out with the hottie who interrupted us last night?>
MaraNara: <Luke. Mmmmm. We're going to

dinner and clubbing after I get off work on Friday.>

Priceless: <So, description.>

MaraNara: <Blond, built, cute little cleft in his chin.>

The phone rang while she was reading Mara's description. She checked the caller ID. Her brother Jason.

"Hi, Jase," she answered.

"Hi, Sissy."

She made a face at the phone. As if "Candy" weren't bad enough, he had to call her by her baby name. Having a baby sister had been such a new experience for her brothers that they just called her "Sister" at first. Later they shortened it to Sissy. Despite her asking them not to, they often—too often for her—slipped up and called her Sissy.

"Can you hold on a minute?" she asked. "I'm talking with Mara on IM and want to let her know I'm taking your call."

"Sure. For a minute."

Yeah, yeah. Busy man.

Priceless: <Sorry, Mara. I've got to go. Price, Price is on the phone.>

MaraNara: <How'd he catch you? Didn't you check caller ID?>

Priceless: <Yeah, but it's after 10 P.M. on a week-

night. I panicked, thinking it might be something with Dad.>

MaraNara: <Everything OK?>

Priceless: <Yeah, but I've gotta sign off. Birthday party stuff.>

MaraNara: <Okay. Bye.>

Priceless: <Bye.>

Candy picked up the phone. "So, what's up?"

"I wanted to check what time you want us there for Dad's birthday."

"Five is good," she answered. He was calling about something else. Unless Jase had undergone a recent personality adjustment, he'd put the time and place of the dinner party for her father's birthday in his Palm Pilot minutes after she'd suggested the idea a couple weeks ago.

"Adam's bringing the cake, right?"

Duh. "Yes." Adam's fiancée, Laura, was a pastry chef at the renowned Gideon Putnam Hotel in the Springs Park in Saratoga. Candy stifled a yawn. She wished he'd get to the point but wasn't sure she wanted to hear it.

"I'll bring the champagne."

"Uh-huh." They'd been over this already too. She stood and started to pace her room.

"T. J.'s got everything set to have the satellite dish installed while we have Dad out of the house."

She knew this. Her oldest brother had called her last Thursday with the details. Jase knew that she knew. She was going to have to ask him outright why he was calling or they'd be on the phone all night chitchatting.

"Yeah, I talked with him last week."

"So, what's the real reason you called?"

"What do you mean?"

She stopped pacing and tapped her toe. "Out with it."

"I wanted to double check the details of the party with you and . . ." He hesitated.

She tapped her toe faster. "And?"

"A friend of mine from law school moved back to Albany a couple of weeks ago."

"He moved *back* to Albany?" Where *had* the poor man been living?

"It was an opportunity to be named VP. The downstate company he works for opened an office in the high-tech park."

She almost understood. A few years up here and he could go back downstate as vice president *or* executive vice president. You had to do what you had to do to get ahead—within reason. And moving to Albany was probably within reason.

"I was telling him about your working with the Burling campaign," he continued.

Sure you were. You were setting me up.

"And . . ." Jase paused. "He'd like to get together with you for a drink or dinner or something. I was telling him about Stephanie's too," he added.

Stephanie's at the Park. Her favorite restaurant. "You didn't promise him anything?" she asked.

"No, I said I'd talk with you. Didn't even give him your phone number."

How thoughtful of Jason, since after the last blind date he set up for her, she told him to never even think about setting her up for another. "Is he newly divorced?"

"Nah, must be a couple years now since he and his wife split."

She went back to pacing. "Any kids?"

"Nope. He's free Friday or Saturday. Like I said, he just transferred here. He's been doing nothing but working."

Nothing but work. She could relate to that. No kids. Divorced a while, so he shouldn't be on the rebound—from the marriage, at least. And dinner at Stephanie's. Her resolve against letting her brothers fix her up was melting.

"What's he look like?"

"About my height, brown hair. Good-looking, like me."

She rolled her eyes at her reflection in the dresser mirror. She'd had to ask. Jase was cute, though, in a serious sort of way. All her brothers were. Her high school friends used to drool over Alex when he was home on college breaks.

"His name?" She really was weakening. But, like she'd just said to Mara, Jase meant well. As long as he wasn't a Harold or a Stanley, getting out and doing something other than serving as Stacie's slave would be fun.

"Andrew—Drew—Bidwell. What do you say?"

She looked at herself in the mirror. Baggy black Northern Lights T-shirt covered with cat hair, red pajama shorts, no makeup, streaky red hair so grown out that it had nothing remotely related to style anymore. Sitting home alone again with no real motivation to be anywhere else. She should have caught up with Mike and Jesse and the others at the tavern after work. *Awk!* Her mind screeched at her reflection. She was turning pear-shaped. Change that. More pear-shaped. She should have left work and caught up with the guys for the soccer game. While Stacie was running her ragged, it wasn't the right kind of running.

"Why not," she heard herself saying into the phone. The guy might not even call. "Give him my number."

Chapter Three

Candy tossed her knockoff Prada bag on the couch and plopped down beside it with an exaggerated sigh.

"That bad?" Mike asked.

"Worse." She groaned. "He was a corporate attorney, some molecular whatever company. Divorced, of course. Seems all my brothers' friends are. Why do I torture myself like this?"

"Good question."

Candy lifted her head from the overstuffed couch to look at Mike, who had settled his long, lean frame into the chair across from her. Was that a touch of sarcasm she caught in his usually sympathetic voice? Like he had any idea of what it was like to grow up with three overachieving older brothers who expected no less of her but, then, did nothing but place obstacles in her way with their overprotection. After all, she was their "baby" sister.

"At least you got a free dinner at Stephanie's," he offered in a more conciliatory tone.

That was more like it. She sighed again, for effect as much as in exasperation. "Free? I paid big time. Believe me."

Mike's raised eyebrow signaled her to continue. What was that about? Like she was going to tell it all to Mike. She picked at a nick in her pomegranate blush nail polish. Why not? She could IM or e-mail Mara later, but IM-ing just wasn't the same as a face-to-face.

"Well, you know, I met him there, at Stephanie's, in case it didn't work out. So he wouldn't be expecting to drive me home."

"Didn't want to get his hopes up?"

"Not really. I just wanted an easy out if it was as bad as most of the dates my brothers set up for me."

"And it was."

"No, it was worse."

Mike put his finger to his lips and tilted his head. It was kind of a girl thing, but not on Mike. On him it was a little sexy.

"You know, maybe you should give these guys more of a chance. No, don't give me that look."

Candy relaxed her brow and held her arguments in check. "What look?"

Mike ignored her question. "Set-up dates are always awkward, like computer dating."

Mike had tried computer dating? Interesting. Of course he and his ex had been together for quite a while. He probably would need a way to get back in circulation. She frowned to herself. He could have asked her.

"Candy?"

"Hmmm?"

"I feel a little sorry for them."

Them? "Oh, my dates." She felt sorry for them too, but she was sure it wasn't the same sorry Mike felt.

"Maybe you should give the guy a second chance. He's a friend of your brother's. You get along with your brothers well enough."

"Yeah, but it's not like I'd want to date one of my brothers."

"Candy." His voice turned stern. "You know what I mean. Bet he's an all-right guy who was a little nervous about the first date."

"Now you're starting to sound like my brothers."

An emotion she couldn't quite decipher flickered in Mike's hazel-brown eyes. "Was the guy rude?" he asked.

She shook her head no.

"Boring?"

"No, although he is pretty focused on his work."

"Mara said you liked that in a man. Thought I was wasting my talents at my job."

Mara and her big mouth. "I might have said something like that. But we're talking about me and my date, not you."

"That, we were. He was ugly, then?" Mike continued his interrogation.

"Nope, he was kind of cute, if a little too serious for me."

Mike fired more questions at her. "He was a chauvinist?"

"No more than most guys.

"The opposite, then. He stuck you with both dinners."

"Don't be silly. He treated."

"I've got it. No spark."

"Actually, we were hitting it off pretty well on the walk here."

His eyes sparked. Then, his lips tightened. "He didn't try something, did he?"

Candy laughed. "Now you really sound like my brothers. He didn't try anything that you wouldn't have tried."

A faint blush tinged Mike's cheeks. Score one for Candy.

"It was the result of his efforts. Blech! Like I was saying, we were walking back here, and I was kind of enjoying myself. We got to the house and I thought maybe I'd invite him in for a beer. I figured you'd have some in the refrigerator. Then . . ." She purposely paused for dramatic effect. "He did it."

"It?" Mike asked.

Again with the questions. "He smashed his face into mine in one of the worst excuses for a kiss I've ever experienced. And I've experienced some really bad kisses."

She waited for Mike's laugh.

"What was wrong with it?" he asked, without a hint of a smile.

"Well, erm . . ." Candy removed another chip of polish off her thumb, avoiding his gaze.

"It's not like I have a sister or anyone to tell me these things." He leaned forward, elbow to knee, jaw to knuckles. "And I have a date with someone new tomorrow night."

A computer date? she wondered. And what was with this uncertainty? "You want all the gory details?" she asked.

"Yeah."

She drew back. He'd asked for it. "We were at the bottom of the front steps. He leaned down. He's about your height. I thought he was moving closer to be heard above a car going by. Then, he was in my face with no warning. Open mouth, wet, mushy. Yuck!

"Too aggressive?"

Was that a humorous twinkle in his eye? She had never noticed how expressive Mike's eyes were before. "Way too aggressive for a blind date, for a not-even-in-the-house-yet kiss."

"So?" His lips twitched. He had good lips, masculine

lips. Not wet. Firm-looking. "The kiss would have been okay if you'd been in the house?"

She threw up her hands and shook her head. "I was being serious."

"Me too." He moved back in the chair and put his ankle across his knee.

As usual, he wasn't wearing socks.

"A guy needs to know these things. Seriously." He responded to the eye roll she gave him. "I know what my ex liked." He half-grinned, then sobered. "But it's been a long time since I've been with anyone else."

"Yeah," Candy agreed. "When you broke up, Mara and Jesse told me they couldn't figure out why you'd stuck it out so long." She cringed at the frown her words evoked. "Sorry. Didn't mean to dredge up bad feelings."

"It's fine. I'm fine."

Yeah, like any guy is fine after his girlfriend ditches him and moves out of state. Mike was a really nice guy. There had to be a way she could help him.

"I have an idea." She sprang off the couch, almost stumbling on the faux Jimmy Choo she'd kicked off after she sat down. Mike grabbed her elbow to steady her, and heat slowed through her arm to her face. Was she blushing? This was *Mike*.

Candy stepped back, fixated on his lips as he tried not to smile. What was with that? She had ideas, good ideas, even if no one—Stacie—seemed to appreciate them.

Candy put her hands on her hips and looked up at him. "Do you want to hear it or not? It could help both of us."

"Sure." He had his lips under control now.

Still, she couldn't help staring at them, especially considering her idea.

"You could use some help getting over your breakup." She waved away any protests he may have had before he could make them.

"And you want me to run interference with your brothers, so they stop trying to fix you up."

Great, if it would work. She sized up Mike. He could be imposing in a tall, lean, no-nonsense way. But he was outnumbered by Price, Price & Price, LLC.

"No, but thanks for the offer. You know what men like, what things about a woman attract them, make then act one way or another toward her."

"Yeah." He was looking south of her face when he answered, making her want to slug him in the shoulder for being such a man. But that's what she wanted—a man's real view—and that was what Mike was giving her.

"And, I know those special things a woman really appreciates and those that can drive her off on the first date." From the dates her brothers had set up, she could probably write a book on the latter.

Mike nodded.

"So you agree?" She prodded, not wanting him to take this as a joke.

"Sure."

"Okay." Her thoughts shot back to her date and its messy ending. "We'll start with kissing," she announced. Jeez, she sounded bossy, but someone had to take charge. "It's an important part of any good relationship."

"Got that covered," he said.

"Be serious. I meant for me." She resisted an urge to punch him in the shoulder. "I am the queen of bad kisses. I must be doing something that brings them on."

The corners of Mike's lips turned up.

"Hey," she said. "You don't want to be acting like my dates if you want to see a woman more than once."

He raised his hands in mock surrender, causing his biceps to flex ever so slightly—and nicely. "What do you want me to do?" he asked.

"Pretend we're at the end of our first date and kiss me."

"Got it."

"You're ready, then?" she asked.

"Oh, yeah."

Candy gave him a look that could have blistered steel. "Okay, give me your best first kiss."

She stood, hands still on hips, feet apart, her baby-blue eyes wide open with demand. Not the demand he usually saw in the eyes of a woman he was about to kiss. This was more like a boxer issuing an all-comers challenge.

Short and sweet, he told himself. Her lips looked so sweet, soft, rosy, and wet with that shiny stuff women used. He tensed as every nerve he had came alive. Next thing he knew, his hands would be sweating. *Short and sweet*, he repeated as a mantra to keep himself in line. Friendly. She was a friend. A friend of a friend.

He bent, lightly touched his lips to hers, and lifted his head waiting for accolades for his gentlemanly conduct.

"That's it?"

Not exactly the reaction he was shooting for. "Didn't want to come on too heavy." Yeah, right. He gave her a once-over from the toes of her strappy sandals, up shapely legs exposed by her clingy dress, to the funny little flip of sunset-red hair, before returning his gaze to her lips. Lips that had been so soft and willing under his.

Exasperation clouded her face. "I wanted you to kiss me like we had just come home from a date—a good date. Not like you were kissing your mother good-bye before heading off to kindergarten."

Kissing his mother? Kindergarten? He'd done what he'd thought she'd wanted. Mike shook his head. She was looking up at him with those baby blues again, and the demand was different this time. Time for him to do things his way.

"Whatever you say." He rubbed her upper arms until she relaxed. Then, he slipped his arms around her waist and lowered his lips to hers, tasting them gently at first, increasing the pressure when she wrapped her arms around his neck and began to kiss him back. This was seriously more like his usual first kisses.

She pulled away, struggling to compose herself. "I

think we went a bit too far." A tinge of pink colored her cheeks. "Was it when I put my arms around you or did I kiss you back too much? How did I encourage you?"

Encourage. That was one way of describing what she'd done to him. "You seemed to like it."

She nibbled on her lower lip in thought and his nerves reentered the alert zone. "I did."

The alert went from yellow to orange.

"I should temper my response," she said as if analyzing one of those voter polls she complained about having to follow for work.

No, she should give in and enjoy. "Want to try it again?"

She had enjoyed it. But there were so many reasons they shouldn't. She fleetingly considered a summer fling. He was awfully cute, and nice. Nope, better stick with her original plan to connect Mike with someone else.

Candy cleared her throat. "Uh, no. I got what I wanted." A hot flush crept up her neck. She stuttered, "I mean, I see better how I can control where a kiss goes. How about you?"

"I think I already knew that."

She playfully slugged him in the shoulder. "You know what I mean. About not overdoing the first kiss, making it just a hint of what it could be."

"Yeah."

"You sound skeptical. For women, kissing is a big part of the relationship. You really should give what I said a try."

He shrugged. A hint of a smile brought out his almost-dimples.

How could she help him get back in circulation if he didn't cooperate? "Wait, I have an idea."

"I liked your other idea." His smile widened to a grin.

She sighed. "So do you want to hear it or not?"

"Sure."

"Okay, go get two nice dishes from the kitchen and I'll be right back."

Candy ran up to her room and grabbed the two bags of candy kisses she had picked up for the volunteers at work. When she came back down, Mike held a blue crystal dish in one hand and a matching pink one in the other.

"Perfect," she said.

"I aim to please."

She looked at him, his broad shoulders, the way his T-shirt hugged his chest, the dark curl that kept falling on his forehead despite his efforts to rake it back. She had no doubt he did.

"Where do you want these?" He waved the dishes in his hands.

"The coffee table is good." After he placed the dishes on the table, she handed him the almond kisses.

"What are these for?"

"To measure our success in applying what we've learned."

"We're having a kissing contest? I could do that."

"Yes, no. Let me explain more."

"Go ahead. The floor's all yours." He sat on the couch and crossed his ankle over his knee.

She sat at the other end. "I read this article about new adult twists to teenage party games in a woman's magazine this afternoon at the nail salon."

He looked at her sadly chipped nails.

"I was waiting for Stacie. She had me drive her so she wouldn't risk her manicure driving herself back to headquarters."

"Of course, part of everyone's job."

"Don't be sarcastic. Do you want to hear me out or not?"

"Sorry, go ahead."

"Basically, you kiss all the men or women at the party and rate each kiss." Candy ignored the grin that spread across his face. "Everyone starts out with a stash of candy kisses. After each kiss, you give the other person his or her rating in candies. Five candies is a perfect kiss and so on down to one candy for barely tolerable—or worse. At the end of the game, the person with the most candy wins.

"Might be fun." He grinned again. "But not exactly conducive to a good relationship."

Candy groaned. If he was going to be like this, trying to help him will be useless. "We'd modify the rules for our purpose."

"Yes, to help improve our relationships."

"Are you always this impossible?"

"Not always. Go ahead, finish."

"So, I go on a date with someone new." *Hopefully, sometime before I hit middle age.* "The first kiss goes exactly as I'd like. I come home and put five plain candy kisses in this dish." She touched the pink dish.

"If the kiss isn't what you expect, you put in fewer candies."

"Exactly. Tonight's would have gotten one candy."

Mike's expression turned thoughtful. "What would you give our kiss?"

Candy finished chipping the polish off the fingernail she'd started on earlier. "Overall, three."

"Three?"

"Well, yeah. The first was silly and the second went too far."

"But you said you liked the second."

She started stripping a second nail. "Yeah, but I would have liked it better as a second kiss."

Mike nodded. "Makes sense. Give them a taste, metaphorically speaking, so they'll want to come back for more. Lots of sense."

They? She'd intended to help Mike find a girlfriend, not help him be a player. What had she started now?

He checked his watch and stood. "I told Jesse that I'd stop by his place for the game—the Sox vs. San Diego. Wanna come?"

"No, thanks." Sheba wandered in and hopped on her lap. She petted her absently, as Mike headed down the hall to his room, tossing the bag of almond kisses in the air and catching them. Sitting around and watching a bunch of grown men trying to hit a little ball with a stick had less appeal to her as a way to spend Friday night than sitting home alone with her cat did. *Sad, so sad.*

"Hey," Mike said when he returned. "What's the winner get?"

"Huh?" She looked up.

"The winner of the kissing contest."

"Candy." She scratched Sheba's soft belly. "Candy."

"Good deal," he said before he whistled his way out.

Priceless: <Mara, you there?>

MaraNara: <Yep, I just had my away message on to screen messages.>

Priceless: <I think I'm making progress on my little summer project.>

MaraNara: <What project?>

Priceless: <Hooking Mike up.>

MaraNara: <Oh, that project.>

Priceless: <We have a competition going.>

MaraNara: <You and your competitions. What's it this time?>

Priceless: <Finding the perfect kiss.>

MaraNara: <And how is that going to help hook Mike up?>

Priceless: <I'm giving him tips on what women want. How to read their signals.>

Sheba jumped up and settle in on Candy's lap. Candy petted her absently.

MaraNara: <He could use some help there.>
Priceless: <I picked up on that during our kissing session.>
MaraNara: <You and Mike had a KISSING SESSION?>

Candy's cheeks flushed. She blamed the heat on Sheba's sleeping on the radiator again. Or was it embarrassment? It couldn't be anything else. Candy shook off that thought too. This was Mara, to whom she had told all for years.

Priceless: <As part of the competition.>
MaraNara: <Sure.>

Even though Mike and Mara had never been more than friends, she still thought Mike was hot. Another wave of warmth flushed through her. Maybe he was right. She was working herself sick. Candy put her hand to her forehead. No temperature.

MaraNara: <You still there?>
Priceless: <Yeah.>
MaraNara: <I've gotta sign off.>
Priceless: <Tall, blond, and built?>
MaraNara: <Yeah, Luke.>

Candy could see the dreamy look on Mara's face, the one she'd always get when she talked about a new man in her life.

MaraNara: <But we gotta talk tomorrow. I wanna know more about this competition and the KISSING SESSION.>
Priceless: <Get off it, Mara.>
MaraNara: <Okay, till tomorrow.>
Priceless: <Bye.>

Candy shut down the computer and petted Sheba. "Mara's got a date and Mike's over playing at Jesse's. It's you and me, girl. Should we watch a movie or call it a night?" Sheba blinked twice, jumped off her lap, and ran out the door.

Abandoned by her cat, even.

Chapter Four

"Candy!" Stacie called from her office.

What now? She looked at her watch and the pile of work on her desk. Stacie knew that she needed to leave early to cook her dad's birthday dinner.

"Would you come back here, please?"

Stacie's almost-pleasant tone put the whole headquarters on alert. Everyone in the room watched Candy skulk back to Stacie's office.

"Close the door." Stacie motioned her to sit.

Candy did, going over the morning in her mind to figure out what had earned her this invitation.

"Am I abrasive?" Stacie asked.

Like industrial-strength sandpaper.

"With men," Stacie added.

Oh, no. Stacie wanted to girl talk. What was with

that? "Well, you were pretty harsh with that man this morning," she said, deciding to be clueless.

"That idiot volunteer who tried to tell me how to run things here?"

"Yep." The guy *had* been overbearing.

"He hit one of my hot buttons," Stacie said.

Not hard to do, in Candy's opinion.

"My father was like that to my mother. He'd yell and expect her to jump."

Why didn't this surprise her?

"I hated it." Stacie broke eye contact and gazed out the window. "I remember hiding in the hall closet, so I didn't have to hear."

Eww. Candy squirmed in the sticky vinyl chair. Too much information. She didn't want to be privy to Stacie's childhood or any other personal information.

Stacie rose from her chair behind the desk, walked around to the front, and sat on the front edge, leaning toward Candy. "Dan asked me to join him on the western New York campaign." Her eyes lit up.

So this was about Dan. Candy hoped he knew what he was getting himself into asking Stacie to accompany him.

Stacie smoothed her wrinkle-free skirt and tapped her finger on her knee. "He wants more media exposure. The travel time will give us an opportunity for strategic planning."

Candy just bet it would.

"Anyway," Stacie's tone turned conspiratorial, "I know I can be brash."

An understatement if Candy every heard one.

"So, I've been working on toning myself down, to practice for the public appearances."

"Since when?" Candy blurted.

Stacie's eyes narrowed. "The past few days, since Dan said he wanted me on the campaign trail."

Candy sneaked a look at her watch. If she told Stacie what she wanted to hear, she might still have a chance to finish her other work and get out of there in time to make the dinner she'd planned.

"Like when my friend Mike stopped in," Candy said.

"Yes."

"You were great," Candy assured her. In a saccharine sort of way. She sent Stacie a pleading look to release her.

Stacie preened and bent closer. "Is he someone special?"

"Hmmm?"

"Mike."

"He's my landlord," Candy answered.

"Oh, yeah?" Stacie's eyes sparkled.

Almost unbelievable. She was sizing Mike up for a campaign contribution. "He only owns a partial interest in the house. His father owns the rest and rents it out, usually to students."

"Oh." Stacie moved back.

"Mike's the property manager for the Housing Alliance," Candy explained. That should chill any thoughts Stacie had of hitting Mike up for money.

Stacie looked blank. “The house you live in is part of this Alliance?”

“No.” Candy laughed. “The Alliance is a nonprofit that provides housing for homeless and disabled veterans.”

“Wait.” The gleam came back to Stacie’s eyes. “Mike’s father is Wheeler Properties, isn’t he? Paul Wheeler.”

“Yes,” Candy answered tentatively, wondering where Stacie was heading.

“It would be a real coup to get his support for Dan. We’re talking big money. Wheeler Properties is the biggest property-holding company upstate.”

Campaign contributions. Of course. “Uh, Mike and his father don’t get along.”

Stacie ignored her. “Any idea where he stands politically? I don’t recall Wheeler being active in local politics.”

“I have no idea what Mike’s father’s politics are. All I know is that Mike has as little to do with him as possible.”

“That’s too bad,” Stacie mused. “You said Mike works with veterans. The veteran vote is important.”

“Homeless veterans. Not a major voting block,” Candy pointed out.

“True. But it would look good for Dan to support housing for homeless vets. Could you set up a tour of one of the houses with Mike?”

Candy fought the urge to roll her eyes. “Mike works with vets because he wants to. He really cares.” And he did, she realized. He’d have to for what they paid him. The guys were important to him.

"He's a vet," she said as if that somehow explained his devotion. "He went into the air force right out of high school and served six years."

"Dan cares too." Stacie's voice grew defensive. "He chose to go to law school and serve his country in the political arena, rather than the military one."

From Stacie, that somehow sounded like a higher calling. Candy swallowed. She'd pretty much said the same to Mike the other day when she got the letter from Albany Law School. *Awk!* Did she and Stacie have more in common than she thought? Was that why Stacie was getting chummy?

"Mike went to business school after the service," Candy blurted, as if sharing that fact made up for how she'd treated Mike the other day.

Stacie nodded. "Exactly. As a businessman, Mike will understand the advantages of getting behind a good man like Dan."

"I'll talk with him," Candy acquiesced. She truly doubted Mike would be interested in being one of Stacie's media events. But if she wanted to get out of here in time to make dinner for five, it was more expedient to not argue.

She looked at her watch.

"You're right," Stacie said.

Candy's attention shot back to Stacie.

"We've got to get going." Stacie went back to her chair and started organizing her papers.

Ah, freedom. Candy stood, more than ready to leave.

"Here." Stacie thrust the pile of papers she had gathered at Candy. "I've made you a schedule for the three days I'll be gone."

Candy reached for pile. It had to be a half a ream of paper.

"You can look over the schedule this afternoon after you finish the supporter thank-you letters. I think I've covered everything."

I'm sure you did and then some.

"You'll see that I've even typed up some tips for handling the unexpected."

Candy nodded and stole another glance at her watch. *Creepy.* It was almost like Stacie was reading her mind. Her thoughts raced ahead. She could read the instructions tomorrow. If she typed fast, she could have the letters all mailed and still be home in time to cook *something* for dinner, if not the roast she'd planned.

"Just a couple more things." Stacie smiled and folded her hands in front of her.

A chill ran up Candy's spine. "Yes?"

"You have your set of keys to the building, right?"

A wave of relief flowed over her. "Sure, in my bag."

"Great. Then I won't have to leave my keys with you to lock up after the volunteers finish."

"You won't be here?" Candy asked.

"No, I have to leave early to pick up a few things and pack. We're leaving first thing in the morning."

"But, but," Candy stammered. "I'm supposed to

leave at two. I asked two weeks ago. It's my dad's birthday. I'm cooking him and my brothers a big dinner."

The last word came out as a whine. Candy didn't care. Maybe it would appeal to Stacie's emotions. Candy gazed hard into Stacie's eyes, looking for a glimmer of sentiment. Then she remembered Stacie's earlier remark about how her father had bullied her mother. She probably didn't do things like birthdays with her father.

"I'm sorry." Stacie almost sounded like she meant it. "I know," she said. "There's this great gourmet restaurant on Lark Street that has takeout." She flipped through her Rolodex. "Here." She handed Candy a card.

Candy stared at the gold script on the card. Her spirits sank with the knowledge that it would be useless to argue. Stacie wouldn't understand that Dad wasn't a gourmet type of guy, that Candy's dinner menu had been pot roast with potatoes, onions, and carrots.

"Ah, thanks." She barely resisted the urge to tear the card into pieces and drop in on Stacie's desk.

"All right, then." Stacie slipped into her rah, rah, motivate-the-masses persona she used with the volunteers. "That just leaves my cat, Cleopatra."

Candy gritted her teeth. She knew what was coming.

"I need you to stop by before and after work tomorrow and a couple of times on Saturday and Sunday to feed and walk her. I'll leave her leash hanging by the back door. My tenant can let you in and out. She lives in the back of the house and is always home."

"Err, couldn't your tenant feed and walk your cat since she's there anyway?"

"Oh, no," Stacie said, her eyes wide in surprise. "I couldn't impose on her like that."

Candy bit her tongue until she tasted blood. "Fine." She clenched her hands in fists at her side, crushing the restaurant card Stacie had given her. "Anything else?"

"No," Stacie answered. "I'll just check on the volunteers' progress with the letter stuffing and be on my way." She opened a desk drawer to get her bag.

Candy escaped the office before Stacie could think of anything else for her to do.

Candy dug her phone out from under the pile of papers on her desk. With the laser printer jamming every few letters, no way was she going to get out of here before four, and that wasn't even considering the time it would take the volunteers to stuff all the envelopes. That could wait until tomorrow. Her dad and brothers would be over about five.

Now, where was the phone book? She glanced around. Oh, yeah, she'd used it to raise her computer monitor. She'd have to look Mike's work number up online since she'd never called him there before. She typed the Housing Alliance information into whitepages.com, absently nibbling on the end of a pen while waiting for the number to appear. When it did she punched the number in the phone.

"Good afternoon, Capital Region Housing Alliance. How can I direct your call?" a woman pleasantly answered.

"Mike Wheeler, please," Candy said.

"I'm not sure Mike's in his office. If he isn't, do you want his voicemail?" the woman asked.

So Mike had an office and voicemail, like any other businessman. She'd always pictured him as more of a maintenance guy, out fixing things. That's the impression Mara had given her, and Mike had never corrected it.

The phone rang repeatedly. *Be there, be there, be there.* She tapped her toe in time with her silent plea.

"Mike Wheeler." His breathless voice came over the phone.

"Mike. I'm glad I got you. I have to ask you a big favor."

"Candy?" he asked.

"Yeah, it's me."

"You just caught me. I was on my way out to the Guilderland vet house. What do you need?"

She released a sigh of relief. "Would you be able to swing by the house on the way and put the roast in the oven for Dad's birthday dinner tonight? I was going to leave at two, but now I'm stuck here until at least four—long story."

"I can do that."

"Thanks. You're a lifesaver. Or at least a dinner saver."

Mike's laugh, deep and somehow calming, warmed her across the line.

"Okay, you need to set the oven at three hundred and twenty-five degrees. You probably should set the automatic shutoff time for six too. It's the dial by the clock."

"I know," he interrupted. "My stove."

Candy cringed. Spending so many hours at work with Stacie was turning her into a know-it-all control freak. She was going to have to do something about that.

"Anything else?" he asked, filling the void in the conversation.

"If it's not too much to ask, can you pick up a jar of beef gravy and a couple bags of salad? I was going to do homemade gravy, along with candied baby carrots, but I guess the quick stuff will have to do. This is so great of you."

"No problem. I have it all under control. I can even greet the guests when they arrive. But Candy?" He paused.

"Yeah?"

"Don't let work make you miss the dinner. Whatever it is can wait until tomorrow."

Mike *was* a really great guy. She smiled. Or maybe he'd heard enough about her dad and brothers to not want to entertain them all evening. "Thanks again. Bye."

"Bye."

She hung up the phone and turned her attention to the laser printer's irritating beep. Another paper jam. At this rate, she'd be lucky to get out of here in time for dessert, which, fortunately, her brother's fiancée, Laura, was bringing.

Mike opened the door to the rich smell of beef roasting, but no Candy. He put her mail on the hall table and walked to the kitchen. You'd think she'd catch on. He'd pointed it out more than once. She had to stop being Stacie's doormat if she was going to have any time for herself. Dedication was one thing; Candy's work situation was something else.

He grabbed a beer from the fridge, twisted off the cap, and made a long shot for the trash can at the far end of the counter. The cap bounced off the tile and into the can. A three-pointer! With the plunk of the cap in the trash, the refrigerator door swung back open. He ought to fix that latch—and buy groceries. His three beers, can of coffee, and carton of half-and-half were huddled together to one side of the lower shelf, overwhelmed by Candy's food on the shelf above. A bag of little carrots and two large red and green peppers perched on the edge as if ready to invade and take over his shelf.

Candy planned to fix the vegetables with her roast if she ever got home. She'd been fussing all week about the dinner. He knew every detail of the menu and more than he wanted to know about every family birthday dinner she could remember. The whole idea of wanting to get together with family—for any reason—was so alien. He couldn't remember his father ever making an effort to be with him for his birthday or any other family gathering. As an adult, Mike reciprocated by avoiding his father no matter what the occasion.

He glanced at the kitchen clock. Four fifty-five. Candy had said she'd be home an hour ago at the latest. He took a long draw of his beer, savoring the cool wetness. Better get to work.

Fifteen minutes later, the roast and the vegetables were back in the oven. Mike left them to cook and settled in the recliner in the living room. He punched on his MP3 player.

Ding dong. The doorbell sounded above the beat of the music. Mike tugged the earphones from his ears. Before he could get out of the chair, he heard the front door open.

"Hello? Sissy?"

By the time he reached the hall doorway, the small entryway was filled with three men who could have been pro linebackers masquerading as lawyers in almost identical conservative suits. Ah, the infamous Price, Price & Price, LLC. He breathed deeply and strode across the threshold, his hand extended.

"Hi." He shook the hand of the nearest Price. "I'm Mike Wheeler."

"I'm T. J. Price and these are my brothers Jason and Alex." The other men nodded a greeting.

"And I'm these oversized lunkheads' father." A smaller, less polished, and more casually dressed version of the brothers pushed past his sheepish-looking sons. "Ted Price." He shook hands with Mike.

"Nice to meet you, sir. Come on in." Mike waved them all into the living room.

Candy's brothers surveyed the room. "You know, we didn't approve of Candy moving in here," T. J. said.

Great. Sounded like he was in for one of those brotherly lectures Candy called the bane of her life. They continued their perusal. So what were they looking for? Kinky sex toys? Mara hadn't exaggerated Candy's brothers' overprotectiveness.

"Ignore them," her father advised. "They have trouble realizing Candy is a grown woman. Where is my girl anyway, in the kitchen cooking? Smells good."

The sound of footsteps on the porch turned everyone's attention back to the door.

Candy. About time. Mike wasn't looking forward to entertaining the Price men. He'd only agreed to dinner because Candy had begged him "to even the odds."

Ding dong.

Who now? Candy wouldn't ring the bell. Mike excused himself and opened the door.

"Hi." A blond in a clingy pink dress smiled up at him. "I'm looking for Ted Price's birthday party." She lifted up the bakery box she held as proof and raked her gaze over him with obvious approval. "Do I have the wrong address?" She actually fluttered her unnaturally long eyelashes.

"Laura." Alex stepped around Mike and took the bakery box. "You've got the right place. Come in. This is Mike, Candy's landlord. My fiancée, Laura."

His fiancée. For a moment he felt sorry for the guy. But, hey, he must know what he was getting himself into.

"Hi, like Alex said, come in." The couple followed him back into the living room.

Ted was coming out of the kitchen. T. J. and Jason had settled into the living room chairs. "Dinner looks like it's about ready," Ted said. "But where's Candy?"

As if on cue, the front door opened and she rushed into the hall scattering the mail from the table to the floor.

"Hi," she called breathlessly as she squatted to retrieve the letters, her slim skirt creeping up to reveal an enticing expanse of tanned thigh.

The back of Mike's neck pricked. He could feel the Price brothers' gazes drilling into him for noticing.

"Sorry I'm so late. I got tied up at work." She gave her dad a big hug. "Happy birthday. I'll have dinner on as soon as I can." She released him and skidded into Jason in her rush to get to the kitchen.

"Sissy." He caught her. "Slow down. Next time Stacie is unreasonable, you've got to assert yourself and just say no."

Mike smiled inwardly. So, he wasn't the only one after Candy to relax some.

"Yeah, they don't pay you anywhere near enough for the time you put in," T. J. added.

"Thanks, guys." She smiled at her brothers and disengaged herself from her Jason's grasp. "The dinner." She pointed in the direction of the kitchen. "Laura, want to bring the cake and give me a hand?"

Laura's mouth formed a pout. She extricated herself from under Alex's possessive arm and sashayed by each of the men to follow Candy.

"Dinner's ready," Mike said.

Candy turned, her face lit with a smile that warmed him to the core. "Like I said earlier, you're a dinner saver."

"A what?" Jason asked.

"A dinner saver." T. J. laughed, making Mike want to smack the smirk off his face. Why did Candy put up with this? Invite it, even, with these family gatherings?

Candy saved him from his more primal instincts by shooting her brother a look that stopped any further comments.

As she marched toward the dining room on her way to the kitchen, she caught her father gazing thoughtfully at her, then at Mike. She wasn't even going to try to figure out what that was about.

Chapter Five

Candy stopped short at the dining room doorway. The table was set with her special holiday tablecloth and the cake pedestal in the center. She owed Mike big time.

"Put the cake there on the holder," she directed. No need to wait and see the confection. Whatever she might think about Laura as a person, she couldn't find any fault with her work.

Candy pushed open the swinging door to the kitchen and breathed in the delicious smell. Her stomach growled, reminding her that she'd had no lunch. But, then, she was only supposed to be working a half-day. She opened the oven, grabbed two pot holders, and lifted the roast out. She was so done with work for the day, for the week, for eternity.

The roast was cooked to perfection with the potatoes and carrots nestled around it just like she'd planned. Mike really was a good friend. To show her appreciation, she should get hopping on connecting him with a nice woman. Somehow the thought depressed her. Maybe she could muster more enthusiasm for the idea once she got through the birthday celebration and she wasn't running on overload.

The door creaked. "Hey, Laura," she called over her shoulder. "Give me a hand with the salad. Everything else looks done. I'll get the bowl. You get the veggies."

"Looks like the salad's ready too." Laura turned and put a big bowl of salad on the kitchen table. "If Mike were my boyfriend, I'd be thanking him royally tonight."

"We're not . . . Mike's just a friend. I rent part of the house from him," Candy said.

"But he's so cute in that earthy, T-shirt and jeans, I-could-use-a-shave way. You know what I mean? That hint of lean muscle rippling under his soft, worn shirt."

Actually, she had noticed those things about Mike. So, why were Laura's comments irritating her so much? Maybe because she half-expected Laura to offer to personally thank Mike? The bigger dig was why that was bothering her, aside from the fact that Laura was her brother's fiancée.

"I thought *GQ* was more your style."

"Well, definitely, for the long term you want to go professional, for security. It's like my investment advisor told me, establish a good core portfolio. Once that's done, you can add some high-risk stocks for fun, to see what they can do. But you can't build a future on those high-risk stocks."

"So, Alex is your core portfolio and Mike could be a high-risk addition to toy with?"

"Something like that."

Candy thought she did well not to pick up the bowl of salad and dump it on Laura's head.

"Don't look at me like that. I wouldn't cheat on Alex." Laura put her hands on her hips and shook her head like Candy were some sort of idiot.

Candy tried to relax her facial muscles into a more neutral expression. She shouldn't brain Laura—not that she had one—she shouldn't.

"Wait," Laura said. "You mean Mike, your not-boyfriend. You thought I was dissing him."

Candy picked up the salad.

"So, what does Mike do? Something manual?"

"He's the property manager for a nonprofit that runs homes for disabled and disadvantaged veterans."

"Like I said, something manual. That's great for keeping those muscles fine-tuned. But where is he going to be in ten years?"

Candy tested the weight of the salad. "Maybe he'll be director, or director of another nonprofit. Mike has a business degree."

"And he's not using it? Worse," Laura decreed. "No drive. The only to get anywhere, have anything is to get on the fast track and stay there."

"Like Alex." Candy lifted the salad a bit higher.

"Yeah, and like you."

She lowered the bowl. Laura was right about her. She wanted to go somewhere, be someone. And she *had* once said something similar to Mara about Mike.

But that was before she knew him. Mike seemed really into helping his veterans. He was as involved with them as he was with the properties he managed. That could lead to something more, couldn't it?

"My advice," Laura said.

Like Candy wanted her advice.

"Would be to enjoy Mike while you're looking for someone better."

"You mean use him?" Laura should know her better than that just because she was Alex's sister, although Candy had had that fleeting thought the other day about having a summer fling with Mike. "We're friends. I wouldn't want to end up hurting him."

"Come on," Laura said, "we're big girls. It's not like he wouldn't be getting something out of it too."

Eww. This conversation was getting as bad as the girl talk with Stacie earlier. Candy had to figure out some nice way to clue Alex into the real Laura, the one that appeared only when he wasn't around.

"Hey." Alex stuck his head in the kitchen. "What are you doing in here? We're hungry." He gave Laura a playful swat on the behind to get her moving. She picked up the salad and carried it into the dining room.

"Need any help with that, Sissy?"

Candy tightened her grip on the iron roasting pan. "Yeah, if you could hold the door open for me."

"Sure thing."

Candy slipped by Alex into the dining room.

"You might want to refill your candy dishes in the living room," Alex said as he let the kitchen door swing shut.

Candy stopped short. The juices from the roast splashed dangerously close to the top of the pan. "You ate the candies in the dish?"

"Yeah, there were only six or seven. It's not like I'm watching my weight or anything." He punched himself in the abs to illustrate the lack of need.

"Six or seven?" Her voice squeaked. She only knew about the three she'd put in the dish Friday when she and Mike had set up the competition. Today was only Tuesday. When had he put the candies in the dish? After the date he'd mentioned having last weekend? She hadn't checked. Were the candies for four kisses? Two kisses? One four-candy kiss?

She looked across the room at him. He grinned, obviously knowing he was driving her crazy because she couldn't ask him about the candies with everyone here. Her brothers would freak if they knew about the kissing competition. Not that it was any of their business. But when had that stopped them before?

"I think it's a bad idea to have candy or other sweets out where you can just grab them," Laura said. "Too easy to come home from a bad day at work and pig out.

Before you know it, all that chocolate's gone to your hips."

Candy plunked the roasting pan on the table with a thud. So maybe she wasn't a size four like Laura, but she didn't have to shop in the plus-size department either. She looked around the table. The men all seemed oblivious to Laura's slight. Maybe she was being too sensitive.

"Sit down," her dad said, pulling out the only empty chair—between him and Mike. "I'll carve the roast."

"You're the guest of honor."

He waved off her protests. "I don't know about your friend here . . ."

Did he put a special emphasis on *friend* or was she just all worked up from Laura's talk and the additional candy kisses?

"But I know these other guys would make a mess of it. And you've done enough putting this party together."

Candy felt a twinge of guilt at how little of the dinner preparation she'd actually done. But she had *planned* everything.

Dad bent and gave her a peck on the cheek. She sat and let him take over.

Candy balanced the creamer in one hand and coffee carafe in the other and pushed open the door between the kitchen and dining room with her hip. So there, Laura, having hips can be useful. Totally!

"Mike," Ted said.

Uh-oh. Family talk was exhausted. Time to grill the nonfamily member. She hoped they wouldn't be too hard on him. Well, maybe a little hard for him not telling her about the kisses.

"Candy tells me you manage veteran housing."

Mike's work. That was a pretty safe subject.

"Veteran and some low-income housing. I work for the Capital Region Housing Alliance."

As she approached the table, T. J. held his cup up for coffee. She set the coffee pot and creamer next to him and sat down. She wasn't about to act as waitress to her brothers.

"How many buildings do you have?" Ted asked.

"Four altogether. Three in Albany. Two of them are big old houses in the Mansion Place neighborhood, and the other is a five-family apartment building in Arbor Hill. The fourth is another apartment building over the city line."

"Will any of them be affected by the proposed zoning change? The one that restricts the number of unrelated people who can live in a house that hasn't been divided into apartments?" T. J. asked. "I read about it in the Albany paper."

Leave it to Price to move the subject to something legal.

Mike tipped his cup back, as if fortifying himself with coffee. He slowly returned it to the saucer. "Yeah, it would put both of the Mansion Place houses out of commission. That's the majority of our housing."

"Tough situation," Ted said.

"Yeah, I don't know where we'd find housing for all of our guys. We have twenty or so residents in the two houses, depending on the day. I'm afraid some would end up on the streets."

This must be the zoning change Mike was checking out the other day when she ran into him at lunch. Why hadn't he talked with her when he found out it could be a problem? She dumped on him about her work all the time. Didn't he know he could do the same with her? He didn't seem to be having any trouble talking about it with her brothers. She shook off the mantle of exclusion that so often settled on her when she got together with her brothers. The protect-little-sister-from-real-life routine got old really fast. Now Mike was doing it too.

"Mansion Place?" Laura piped in. "I hear it's going to be one of *the* places to live in the city, once the skeezy people are out."

Jeez. How did Alex put up with her? More than that, why? Sure, she was drop-dead gorgeous. But he could do so much better.

"Laura, some of those skeezy people are Mike's veterans." Candy bit her tongue. She glanced at Mike. His expression was unreadable. Her heart sank. She'd sunk to Laura's level. "They'd have no place else to go," Candy finished lamely.

Laura's face shouted, "So?"

The *bring* of a cell phone stopped the conversation and sent her brothers and Mike scrambling.

"It's mine," Mike said. "Yep, yeah. I'll be there." He snapped the phone closed. "There's a plumbing problem at the Madison Ave. property."

"Need any help?" Ted asked with a little too much enthusiasm in his voice.

Nothing was going right today. Why had she even bothered with the party? They hadn't even told her dad about their birthday gift yet, and he was ready to jump up and leave to fix a broken toilet or something.

"I have my tools right out in my truck," Ted added.

"Naw, it's okay. It's nothing I haven't handled before. Stay for the rest of your party."

Her father had the good grace to not look too disappointed with Mike's refusal. What was it about men? Didn't they have any ability to pick up on people's feeling?

She turned so her dad couldn't see her face and mouthed a "thank you" to Mike. He responded with an arched eyebrow.

Except Mike. Where had he learned to pick up on feelings? Maybe she could send the men in her family there. Stacie too, and maybe Laura, for Alex's sake.

Mike stood. "Since you might be gone when I get back, it was nice meeting you."

"Same here," Jason said.

"Yeah, nice meeting you," T. J. said, and Alex nodded.

"I feel good knowing you're here with Candy," Ted said. "I used to worry about her down here in Albany, all by herself. I won't now."

That brought a round of nods from her brothers, meaning what? She'd always had a roommate. But never a male roommate. What chauvinists—and hypocrites. Until today, not one of them, except her dad maybe, approved of her living here. Were they more intuitive than she'd given them credit for? Had they somehow picked up that Mike wouldn't hit on her? And why not? Not that she wanted him to. Well, remembering the kiss, maybe a little bit. She was experiencing a mega dry spell in the dating department. A brief rain shower, even from someone like Mike who was strictly a friend could give her a boost.

"Earth to Sissy," T. J. said. "We could use some more coffee."

She blinked. Mike was gone. T. J. was holding the empty coffee carafe out to her.

"Are your legs broken?" she asked him.

"But you're already up."

It wasn't worth arguing about. She took the carafe and went to the kitchen to refill it, wondering how long Mike would be gone. He had some explaining to do about those kisses Alex had eaten.

The wall phone rang. Candy tried to ignore it. All she needed to make her day complete was Stacie calling from Rochester with something she needed done right away. The ringing stopped and started again. She stopped. *The satellite people. It could be them.* She'd forgotten they were going to call when the installation was done.

"Hello."

"Candy? This is Dave."

"Hey, Dave." She'd gone to high school with Dave Ivy. His father owned the satellite company. "You all done?"

"Yep, everything's all set in time for tonight's Red Sox game."

"Thanks. Bye." She hung up. Dad wouldn't ditch the party for baseball, would he? She hadn't really had a chance to talk just with him all evening.

She and the carafe returned to the dining room.

"I heard the phone," Jason said. "Anyone we know? Drew, maybe?"

"Drew?" T. J. and Alex latched on the name like a dog on a bone.

"Friend of mine. Candy went out with him this past weekend."

Arrgh. Jase must have talked with Drew. "We went to dinner."

"So, you'll be seeing him again?" Jase asked.

"No, he seemed like a nice guy, but not my type."

"When are you boys going to learn not to set Candy up with your lawyer friends?" Ted asked. "Despite what you think, she doesn't need to marry a lawyer to be a success."

Candy caught a look of disbelief on Laura's face. She had real concerns for Alex.

"Thanks, Dad. Why would I need to marry a lawyer,"

she asked her brothers, "when I could be one myself, instead?"

"Meaning?" Jase asked.

"I applied to Albany Law School."

"What?" blasted back in quadrosonic sound.

"Candy, why'd you do that? I thought you were happy with your PR work, your boss excepted," Ted said.

She read between the lines: *not another career change.*

"I am, Dad." She defended herself. "I like PR and politics even better. But, if Dan loses, I'll be out of a job. Law school is my fallback."

"I don't see it. Why do you need to start all over again? Albany is the state capital. There are other jobs."

"Like I said, I like the politics. A law degree could help me there."

"It's my fault, Dad," Alex said over her explanation.

His admission earned him her dad's "you're in deep doo-doo" look.

"I fixed Sissy up with one of my lawyer friends, a guy we all know. Afterward, she said he was a jerk, that if he could get through law school, anyone could. And I said prove it."

Ted groaned. "Candy, don't do it to just to prove your brothers wrong. They're all idiots anyway. Just because they have law degrees doesn't mean they're smart."

“I won’t, Dad. I’m just thinking about it.”

“So, who *was* on the phone?” Jase asked.

They never let up. It could have been a boyfriend, or Stacie, or Mara, none of which he needed to know.

“Dave.”

“All right!” Alex said.

Ted tilted his head toward her, his eyes questioning.

“No Dad, not a new boyfriend. Dave Ivy. For your birthday, we got you a satellite dish. Dave called to let us know it’s all set.”

Her father’s face lit up with surprise. “Thanks, guys,” Ted said. It’s too much, but I’ll take it anyway.” He glanced at his watch. “If I leave now, I could be home for the Sox game.”

He was going to do it. Leave his party for a baseball game.

“You don’t mind, do you, Candy?”

What could she say? “No, Dad, we’ve had the cake. The party is pretty much over. You go home and enjoy your present.” She walked him to the door and gave him a big hug.

He hugged her back. “Thanks for the dinner and everything.” He stepped away. “And I liked your friend Mike.”

So, Daddy liked her new friend. She’d always be his little girl. Not much she could do about that. “I’ll talk with you next week.” She waved him off.

“I told you the party wouldn’t last that late.” Laura’s

words greeted her return to the dining room. "We can still make the movie."

Alex smiled sheepishly. "She really wants to see it."

"Go ahead." She could do without Laura's further company.

"We'll help you with the dishes, Sissy," Jase said.

She started to say no, then stopped herself. She could use some help, and they owed her for all her trouble.

"What do you want to do with this?" Jase held up the champagne he'd brought.

Leave it. I could use some—or all—of it, Candy thought to herself. "Take it back with you," good sister Sissy said.

"Naw, Jase, leave it here," T. J. contradicted. He smiled at her. "Keep it until you have something to celebrate. When Dan wins, if not before."

She smiled back. "Okay. You guys bring the dishes and I'll load them in the dishwasher. You wouldn't be able to fit in half as many dishes as I can, and I don't want to be up all night running and reloading the dishwasher."

"Yes, ma'am," Jason said.

T. J. nodded. "We defer to your superior homemaking skills."

Candy laughed. "Go!" She pointed at the door to the dining room.

Once they'd finished the cleanup and her brothers had left, Candy went up to her room and turned her computer on. "Hey Girl," it called to her. Mara was online.

Priceless: <Hey.>
MaraNara: <Hey yourself. Party over?>
Priceless: <Yep. Dad had to hurry home to check out the Sox game.>
MaraNara: <Bad?>
Priceless: <No, yes.>
MaraNara: <Price, Price & Price, LLC?>
Priceless: <And Stacie and Laura.>
MaraNara: <What happened?>
Priceless: <To start, Stacie dumped a bunch of work on me so that she could take off with Dan for his campaign tour in western New York.>
MaraNara: <Ooooo, Stacie and Dan again.>
Priceless: <Forget them. I was supposed to leave early so I could cook Dad's dinner. Instead, I was there all day and had to stop and feed Stacie's cat.>
MaraNara: <Bitter?>
Priceless: <Way bitter. Mike ended up cooking dinner.>
MaraNara: <Interesting.>
Priceless: <It get more interesting. Just when I'm feeling all warm and fuzzy about Mike's thoughtfulness.>
MaraNara: <Warm and fuzzy?>

Priceless: <Knock it off. You know what I mean.>
MaraNara: <Sure I do. ☺>
Priceless: <I find out Mike's been adding kisses to the candy dish.>
MaraNara: <That ruined the party for you? This is interesting.>
Priceless: <No, it frustrated me.>
MaraNara: <Even more interesting.>
Priceless: <Because I couldn't ask him about the kisses in front of everyone. Then, Laura gave me a private lecture on how I should use Mike as my boy toy for the summer.>
MaraNara: <So, are you going to?>
Priceless: <No!!!!!>
MaraNara: <Just kidding. How can Alex stand her?>
Priceless: <Not a clue. She also advised me to avoid chocolate. Goes right to the hips, you know.>
MaraNara: <Does not!>
MaraNara: <So, then, why are you online?>
Priceless: <???>
MaraNara: <Instead of grilling Mike?>
Priceless: <He got called away from dinner for some emergency at one of the houses.>
MaraNara: <Typical.>
Priceless: <Right after I called some of his guys skeezy.>
MaraNara: <!!>

Priceless: <Not on purpose. I was trying to correct Laura.>

MaraNara: <Uh-huh.>

Priceless: <I was! It was all about some zoning problem he's having.>

MaraNara: <He told you about a work problem?>

Priceless: <No, Jase brought it up. Something he'd read in the paper.>

MaraNara: <More like it.>

Candy was picking up a trend here. Sounded like Mike didn't share work with Mara either. That knowledge lifted her spirits.

Priceless: <I'm thinking I should talk to Dan about the problem. Get him behind the Housing Alliance's effort to keep their houses open. Supporting veteran housing is smart politics.>

MaraNara: <Bad idea, all round.>

Priceless: <??>

MaraNara: <I've got to spell it out?>

Priceless: <Yeah. I think it could help everyone.>

MaraNara: <One, Mike doesn't like anyone helping him.>

MaraNara: <Two, sounds like a local issue, not a state issue.>

MaraNara: <Three, if Dan does buy in, Stacie will take all the credit. No benefits for you.>

Priceless: <Don't hold back.>
MaraNara: <What are friends for?>
Priceless: <With friends like you . . . >
MaraNara: <You don't need anyone else? Only trying to help, really. Save you some grief.>
Priceless: <Yeah.>
MaraNara: <But you're going to do it anyway.>
Priceless: <Well, yeah.>
MaraNara: <Promise me you'll think it out first.>
Priceless: <Promise.>
MaraNara: <Cross your heart?>

Mara would invoke their childhood pledge, the one Candy's mother had taught them.

Priceless: <Cross my heart.>
MaraNara: <Okay. Hey, I gotta go. Early morning meeting tomorrow.>
Priceless: <Bye, then.>
MaraNara: <Bye.>

Candy looked at the clock. Nine forty-five. *Sigh.* Mara must have something going on that she wasn't sharing. Early morning meeting or not, she couldn't imagine her friend going to bed this early—unless she wasn't alone. Irritation flared. Mara could have said that. She could handle Mara wanting to be with Luke, rather than IM-ing with her. But not saying so grated on her nerves. Why were people being so closemouthed with her? First Mike, now Mara. Mara didn't have to hide her love life just because she didn't have one. It was like everyone she knew was taking cues from her brothers and trying to protect her from the realities of life.

She clicked on Spider Solitaire, keeping an ear open for Mike returning.

Chapter Six

"Hey."

Mike looked up from the piece of birthday cake he was scarfing down. "Want some?" He pointed toward the refrigerator. "There's another piece left."

"No, I had enough at dinner." She sat down across the table from him. "Did you get your problem taken care of?"

He stopped midbite. "Oh, the toilet. Yeah."

She slapped the table. "I knew it was a toilet."

He arched a brow.

"I did," she insisted. "And I knew that Dad would want to come help if it was."

"He likes to fix toilets? I'll keep that in mind."

"You've got to know him. He's a plumber, retired

before he wanted to. Thanks for discouraging him from coming with you."

"No problem. Was he surprised about the satellite dish?"

"So much so that he had to rush home to catch the Red Sox game. As soon as he left, Laura hustled Alex off to some show it sounded like she would have gladly skipped the dinner for."

"I can see Laura hustling."

"Mike!" She crumpled a napkin from the holder and tossed it at him.

He caught it and wiped his face. "Thanks. I'm sorry if my call broke up your party."

"Oh, no. It didn't. You didn't. I should be thanking you. There wouldn't have been a dinner at all if you hadn't cooked it."

Mike picked up his plate and fork and carried them to the sink. "You would have done the same."

"Correction. In the same situation, I would want to do the same, but something would interfere and I wouldn't be able to."

He turned back to her laughing. "Yeah." His eyes crinkled at the corners and laugh lines bracketed his lips. The lips that had put those four additional kisses in the candy dish.

He leaned toward her, resting his forearms on the top of the ladder chair. Her heart quickened. Laura was right about one thing. Mike was awfully cute, which was probably how he'd added those kisses so quickly—without any help from her.

One side of his mouth turned up as if he could hear what she was thinking.

She tore the napkin in half and blurted, "Was it four one-candy kisses? One four-candy kiss? Two two-candy kisses?"

He scratched his head.

"The candies that Alex ate. Out with it."

Ring! Ring! The phone interrupted.

It was almost midnight. "Who could that be?" she said as much to herself as to Mike.

"Stacie," they answered in unison.

"Don't answer it," Mike said.

"It could be about Dad." The phone in the kitchen *would* have to be the only one in the house without caller ID. But she'd never forgive herself if she didn't answer and it turned out her father had had another heart attack.

She picked up the receiver. "Hello."

"Stacie?" Mike mouthed.

She nodded.

He pointed to the door, signaling he was leaving.

Candy tightened her grip on the receiver. "Yes, Stacie." She was going on about the reception she and Dan had attended in Rochester. Ordinarily, Candy would have been mildly interested. The western New York vote was important to the campaign. But as Stacie droned on, all Candy could think about were those kisses.

Candy looked at the alarm clock. Eight fifteen. She'd overslept big time. She never overslept. How was she going to get over to feed Cleopatra then to headquarters in time to open for the morning volunteers? Maybe Mike. She strained to hear any sound of him downstairs. No, he'd done far too much for her already. Of course, he did slip out last night without answering her kiss question. She threw some clothes on and ran down the stairs.

"Mike." No answer. She stuck her head in the kitchen. It was empty. If Mike were already gone, Cleopatra would just have to wait until lunchtime. She let the door go and it just missed catching Sheba's tail. The cat wrapped herself around Candy's legs and meowed.

"Poor kitty." She squatted and picked up Sheba. Here she was all concerned about getting to Stacie's to feed her cat and she hadn't even given Sheba her breakfast—or last night's dinner, that she could remember. Maybe Mike had?

"Meow," Sheba chastised her. Candy petted her ruffled fur and carried her into the kitchen. At the shake of the cat food box being lifted from the cupboard, Sheba catapulted to the floor, using Candy's side as a springboard. The feline skidded to a stop in front of matching food and water dishes sitting on a rubber mat. Mara had gotten it somewhere and given it to Sheba as a Christmas gift last year.

"Hang on, pretty kitty." As she filled the food dish to the top, Candy made a mental note to bring a treat home for Sheba. While the cat crunched, she filled the water dish and put the cat food away. Then she dashed back upstairs to finish getting ready for work. A glimpse in the mirror at the top of the stairs reminded her that she still hadn't managed to fit a haircut in.

Minutes later, makeup on, hair combed, she raced down the stairs to the door. The empty candy dishes in the living room seemed to mock her as she passed. Unlike Mike, she hadn't managed to fit in any kisses, either.

Candy and the bus arrived at the corner at the same time.

"Do you have your lunch?" she heard a young woman about her age ask the little girl beside her.

"Yes, Mommy," the girl answered.

"I'll pick you up at camp after work," the woman said.

"Okay. Can we have mac and cheese for dinner?"

The woman nodded.

"Yippee, yippee!" The little girl gave her a big hug and kiss and skipped up the bus steps to a teen in a Y-camp T-shirt.

Candy followed and took a seat behind two other

teens. The boy had his arm draped around the girl's shoulders.

"Did you do all those math problems?" He nibbled on her ear.

"As many as I could. There must have been like a hundred." She turned so that her lips welded to his.

After a minute or so of upfront and personal, Candy shifted her attention to the buildings streaming by the bus window. When she turned back, the couple was still at it.

Jeez, the kiss was up to ten candies on length alone, even if it were lacking in finesse. If they'd put half as much effort into math as into each other, they wouldn't have to be going to summer school.

The bus slowed for the next stop—the high school—and the pair disentangled themselves to pick up their backpacks. Arms wrapped around each other, they trailed behind a few other teens leaving the bus, pausing several times on their way to smile at each other and steal another quick kiss.

Candy slumped in the seat feeling old and tired. And her day hadn't even really begun yet.

She got off two stops later, undecided whether to try boosting her energy with a dash to Starbucks for a caramel latte or head right to work. The bus pulled away belching diesel fumes behind it. A sleek silver sedan took its place. Candy stepped back to avoid being hit by the car door as it swung open. A middle-aged woman backed out, taking an inordinate amount of time to kiss the car driver good-bye.

Oblivious to Candy standing right behind her, the woman adjusted the shoulder strap on her large Coach bag, almost smacking Candy with it. The woman smiled and blew another kiss at the man in the car before she headed toward the boutique facing the bus stop.

Kissy, kissy, kissy. Young, old, everyone was getting off to a sweet morning but her. Candy decided that Starbucks wouldn't help. She'd probably get to the coffee shop only to find that all they had left was bitter herbal tea and no Equal. Maybe she ought to talk with Mike about revising her part of the kissing competition. Let her log in any kisses she saw, since that was probably as close as she was going to get to any actual kissing.

"Candy? Is zat you?" the thickly accented voice asked.

"Andre!" she greeted her elderly former neighbor.

"I have not seen you since you move from zee building. How have you been? Let me look at you." The French Canadian took her hands in his and kissed her soundly on both cheeks.

Candy fleetingly wondered if she could count the kisses in the competition. At least she was participating in these kisses, not just viewing them.

"You are beautiful as always," he said.

She kissed his leathery cheeks in return. "Thanks. I really needed that this morning."

"Can you join me for a coffee?" he asked.

"I'm sorry. I really shouldn't. I have to be at work."

His smile crumpled. "I understand."

But she didn't have to stay at work. Stacie wasn't there. Her day brightened considerably. She could duck out for some coffee once she opened up. "I'd love to have coffee with you. You go ahead and I'll meet you in five minutes. I just have to unlock headquarters for the others."

He beamed. "I will order something for you. A surprise."

"Five minutes." She raised her hand to him, fingers spread.

Headquarters would be fine without her for an hour. It wasn't like she didn't put her weekly time in and then some. Candy's conscience—or, maybe, fear Stacie would call while she was out—compelled her to reassure herself. She jingled the keys and picked up her pace, surprised at how much she was looking forward to coffee with Andre. Even though he was old enough to be her grandfather, it was the best offer she'd had in a long time.

This was one date she'd enjoy. And it *was* a date, she insisted to herself. It met the general criteria. A man asking a woman to go somewhere with him, or in this case meet him somewhere. And, since it was a date, she could count Andre's kisses—especially since she couldn't see any more coming her way any time soon. They would at least put her in the competition, although she'd still be down two candies to four. She couldn't in good conscience give Andre's welcome more than one candy for each kiss. But maybe he'd give her a peck on the cheek good-bye and bring her up to three.

Forty-five minutes later, she walked into headquarters to be greeted by pandemonium—or as much pandemonium as a group of four could generate. One was rummaging in the supply cabinet. Another was gesticulating wildly to someone on the phone. Candy's heart stopped. Stacie, most likely. A third was moving water-soaked boxes of letterhead, she hoped, not finished letters, out of the way of a torrent of water flowing from the ceiling above. Foot for foot, Stacie's planned visit to Niagara Falls today had nothing on the water display Candy was witnessing.

"Here." The woman on the phone shoved it at her.

"Hello."

"Candy?" Stacie's voiced scratched like fingernails on a chalkboard. "What is going on there?"

"I—"

"Whoever answered the phone seemed to think you weren't there. Are you working in my office?" Stacie demanded.

"I—"

"You know that you shouldn't let just anyone answer

the phone. We have an image to maintain for potential donors."

"I—"

"I'm waiting. You haven't told me what's going on. What's all that noise?"

"Stacie, chill." Oh, my God. Had she really just told Stacie to chill? Hey, it seemed to have worked. The receiver was silent. "There's a water leak from upstairs. I've got to help move the boxes of letterhead out of the way. I'll call you when we're done."

"Letterhead, not letters, right?" Stacie screeched. "You did get the letters out yester—"

Candy lunged for the phone cradle and successfully cut Stacie off midword.

What a mess. She tried to avoid the stream of water as she walked to the back of the room to help move the boxes. "Anybody know what happened?" she asked.

The volunteer who was rummaging in the supply closet returned with a plastic garbage can and a mop.

"It started as a slow drip. Then the ceiling tiles came down and . . ." She nodded upward as she stuck the can under the flow. "We called the management company. They sent someone to check it out. He's upstairs now. We tried knocking on the upstairs apartment door, but no one answered."

"Well, let's finish moving these boxes and mop up." Candy slid her fingers into side handles of a box that looked relatively untouched by water and lifted. Another ceiling tile came down, giving the water a new outlet. Water streamed into the box. The bottom gave way and the finished letters fell to the floor with a plop, soaking her flip-flops.

She jumped back, emitting a watery squeak. "Whoever management sent doesn't seem to be helping. Have you saved any of the letters?"

"Most of them, actually," the woman with the mop answered.

The fact that staying later than planned yesterday hadn't been a total waste somewhat calmed Candy's urge to throw the dripping-wet letters into the air and laugh hysterically. She squished her way over to retrieve the last box in danger of the deluge. It stayed intact.

"Candy," her fourth volunteer called.

"Yeah?"

"The maintenance guy wants to talk with you."

She glanced over her shoulder as she maneuvered her box to the saved letters collection. The guy she glimpsed looked familiar. Dark hair, patrician profile, wiry build. Mike? Had he come to save her once more? She really ought to get him his own superhero cape.

"I'll be right there." She added her box to the pile and fluffed her hair before turning for a better look. No, this guy was much younger, teenish, but the resemblance was uncanny. She joined them in the vestibule.

"Ma'am," he started.

Ma'am? He wasn't *that* much younger than her.

"I fixed the problem. Sorry it took so long."

A chill ran through her. His voice and mannerisms were Mike's too.

"Someone locked and shut the bathroom door with the tub faucet running," he explained. "Had to take the door off the hinges. That's what took me so long."

"Thanks. I'm glad you fixed it before we had any more damage."

"About the damage, the tiles and stuff." He fidgeted as if not sure whether he should continue. "You should call the management company to send someone else out to fix them once everything dries."

"I'll do that."

"Anything else?" He eyed the door as if planning his escape.

She was staring. She knew she was staring. He was like a teenage Mike. "Yeah. You look just like someone I know. Are you related to Mike Wheeler?"

"Mike? Sure. We're cousins." He visibly relaxed. "In fact, I'm working for his dad until I start classes at Rensselaer Polytech the end of August. Uncle Paul owns this building. But you must know that."

"Wheeler Properties owns the building?" That was news to her. News to Stacie too, since she'd looked at Mike as a connection to his father for campaign contributions.

"Naw," he answered with the nonchalance of a very young adult. "One of his other companies owns some of the properties right in Albany. He has a couple companies for tax purposes or something."

"That explains it." Yeah, clear as mud. Paul Wheeler had other property companies? Stacie, who made a point of know everything, didn't know he was their landlord?

"I gotta go. Another call. Nice meeting you . . . ?"

"Candy." She held out her hand in greeting. "I live with Mike at the Elm Street house."

"Mike always did have good taste." He gave her an appreciative once-over.

The thrill his compliment gave her was too enjoyable to ruin it with a correction. She *did* live at the house with Mike, just not *with* him.

"I'm Matt. You tell Mike I said hey."

"Sure thing. And thanks again."

Candy returned to the main room and, in a very Stacie-like manner, clapped her hands. "Let's get the mess cleaned up and those letters stuffed. I'll make a list of the batches that have to be reprinted." Hey, she was in charge. No reason not to take the best work for herself. She pulled the soggy ID sheets from the water-damaged boxes and took them with her to Stacie's office and the better printer.

A few computer clicks later, and the printer was humming along, spitting out thank-you letters. She flipped Stacie's Rolodex to the management company's card and situated herself more comfortably in her Aeron chair, provided courtesy of the campaign, of course. Everyone else, Candy included, had to make due with ancient desks and chairs picked up at a state auction of old office equipment.

A familiar icon on the screen caught her eye. Stacie had Instant Messaging. Who would have guessed? Candy looked at the clock and back at the icon. Why not? She clicked and logged in. Her buddy list popped up. Darn it. Mara wasn't online. She double clicked on MaraNara in the offline list.

Priceless: <Hello! I could use you here.>

While she waited for a response from Mara, Candy Googled the name of the management company. Pages of search results appeared. She sifted through them until she came to a link to BIZLEADS in classified pages of the *Albany Business News*. Another mouse click took her to the newspaper page.

Mansion Place Management Company to Wheeler Properties, Loudonville Road, Latham, NY

There it was in black and white. Mike's father was campaign headquarters' landlord. She sent the page to the print queue and refined her search to include the word *zoning*. The pages of results shrunk to four links, two to *Times Union* news stories, one to a *Business News* story and one to a Web site called Vets Alive.

She clicked on the link to the Web site first. The

screen radiated anger in its flashing red and black graphics and in the faces of the men and women accompanying the equally heated comments. She wondered if any of them were Mike's "guys." Another link at the bottom took her to a copy of the proposed zoning change. She clicked the printer icon and started reading online while she waited for the pages to print out.

"Candy?" One of the volunteers stood in the doorway. "Are the new letters printed yet? We've finished the others."

Candy realized that the hum of the printer had stopped. She'd been so engrossed in research that she hadn't noticed. "Yes, they just finished." She hoped her statement didn't sound as false as it felt. "Let me get my, ah, report from the bottom of the stack and you can take them.

Candy walked to the printer without making eye contact with the woman. Jeez, you'd think she'd been doing something illegal to generate all this discomfort, rather than something that could help the campaign. Getting behind a veterans' group couldn't be a bad thing. She flipped through the papers until she found the first page of the zoning proposal, making a point of letting the woman view the page title, so she'd see Candy was working on something official—sort of.

"Here you are." Candy handed her the stack. "There weren't as many as I feared. One of the damaged boxes was defective letters that I had already reprinted yesterday."

"Great. We'll let you know when we finished."

"Thanks." Candy returned to the computer and clicked on one of the *Times Union* articles. Holy cripe, the management company was way involved in the proposed zoning change. She printed the three news stories.

The messaging window popped open.

MaraNara: <I'm here. But not for long.>
Priceless: <You won't believe this.>
MaraNara: <Try me.>
Priceless: <It looks like Mike's father is trying to zone him out of a job.>
MaraNara: <??>
Priceless: <You know that zoning problem I told you about?>
MaraNara: <The one I told you not to get involved in?>

Candy ignored Mara's comment.

Priceless: <Mike's father has a second property management company, not Wheeler, that has a big interest in Mansion Place properties. The zoning change would benefit him big time.>
MaraNara: <I believe it. I've met his father. A real skeeze. IMO.>
Priceless: <What do you think? I'm putting this

stuff together for Dan and Stacie and Mike, if he doesn't already know.>
MaraNara: <Trust me he knows. Don't go there.>
Priceless: <But for Dan and Stacie. This could be a good campaign cause.>
MaraNara: <Nope.>

Mara was too apolitical. She couldn't see the power in this. Mike would. He must deal with politics all the time on his job.

Priceless: <I'll talk to Mike first.>
MaraNara: <Bad idea.>
Priceless: <Just talk.>
MaraNara: <Don't say I didn't warn you.>
Priceless: <☺>.
MaraNara: <Don't go there.>
Priceless: <Back off. I get the idea.>
MaraNara: <Oops. Break's over. Gotta go answer more customer service e-mails. Talk to you later.>
Priceless: <Later.>
MaraNara: <Bye.>

Candy gathered her pages from the printer and reread them. She was right; Mara was wrong. Getting Dan and Mike together on the veteran housing/zoning issue couldn't be anything but good for everyone.

"We're done." The volunteer was standing in the doorway again. "Want me to stay until the mail gets picked up?"

"No. You guys can all go. I'll come out and wait. Let me turn the computer and stuff off first."

Candy walked back to the main room and looked around. Except for the missing ceiling tiles, you'd hardly know anything had happened.

"You guys are great," she said. "When I talk with Stacie and Dan, I'll let them know what you all did today."

Speaking of Stacie, she looked at her watch. It was three hours since she'd hung up on her. Stacie and Dan must be having a good time touring the falls. Ordinarily, Stacie would have checked in at least twice.

"Bye."

"See you."

"Later."

"Bye, and thanks again," Candy said as the volunteers filed out.

She sat at her desk and reached for the phone. It was still off the hook and should be making that annoying "beep, beep, beep," alarm signaling it was off the hook. The phone service must be out, or shorted out by the water. Her gaze lifted to the lights above. They were on, but should they be? She could hear the evening news: *Flames from electrical fire engulf gubernatorial candidate's headquarters, trapping media assistant inside.* Maybe she should cart the letters over to the post office rather than wait for the mail carrier. She'd write her report for Stacie and Dan and Mike at home.

Candy eyed the boxes of finished letters. It would take her at least three trips to the post office to get them all out. Her gaze returned to the lights. They weren't sputtering or sparking or hissing. They must be fine. And having no phone service here put her out of touch with Stacie. Never a bad thing.

She turned on her computer and went to work on the report.

Chapter Seven

"Nice!" Mike greeted her, his gaze raking her head to toe and back again.

Her heart thumped a staccato beat. Anger. Anger and frustration. That had to be it. Why else would her pulse be racing?

Pushing back the rain-soaked lock of hair that was plastered to her forehead, Candy glared at him. "Yeah, to borrow a phrase from my mother, I'm striving for that look-what-the-cat-dragged-in look." And considering what she'd just gone through with the not-so-lovely Cleopatra, that wasn't far off the mark.

She marched over to the couch, whipped open the coffee table drawer, and pulled out the plain candy kisses. She plunked three into her candy dish for her "date" with Andre and weighed whether to replace the ones from Mike's kiss that Alex had eaten, then decided not to.

Mike eyed her intently. "So, did you go for the new look to procure the kisses or is it a result?"

"Funny." She fell back on to the couch.

He reached down, reopened the coffee table drawer, and drew out four almond kisses. "To replace the ones Alex ate." He dropped them in his dish and grinned. "What happened?"

"What didn't?"

He raised his brow in that way he did.

"I overslept, which I never do. All the way to work people were . . . never mind." She waved her words off. "Then, getting off the bus, I ran into an old friend."

Mike eyed the candy dish. "That was a bad thing?"

"No." She favored him with what she hoped was a secretive, seductive smile. Let him contemplate those kisses. "But while we were having coffee, all hell broke loose at headquarters."

"Stacie returned early?"

"No, not that bad." Candy couldn't help laughing. "The people in the apartment upstairs left the bath tub faucet running. The tub overflowed and rained down on us. Knocked out some ceiling tiles and everything."

"Right on you? You're all right? Why didn't you come home and clean up and change?"

She wiped her dirty hands on her equally dirty skirt and pushed her wet hair back again. "This"—

she gestured down herself—"is not from the water leak. Cleopatra got out when I stopped at Stacie's after work to feed her. "This"—she gestured again—"is from scaling the fence into the alley to chase her down and getting caught in the downpour that just stopped."

The corners of Mike's mouth started to curve up.

"Don't you laugh. It wasn't funny."

The muscles around his mouth tightened in his effort to keep a straight face.

"Okay, laugh. Get it out."

"No, you're right. It's not funny," he choked out before he collapsed back in the chair in laughter.

She glared at him.

"Sorry." He glanced around the room like a drowning man looking for dry land. "So, what happened at headquarters? With the leak."

"The water came down in torrents all over the letters we had ready to send out."

"All of them?" He reached over and patted her knee, right above the oil streak and below the rent in her skirt.

She pulled back. Where was this touchy stuff coming from? Her coffee with Andre? No, this was Mike, Mara's forever-friend Mike, her landlord Mike. She studied his face. No clue there, just his usual friendly expression.

"Not all the letters. Maybe about a third. We still were able to get them all out today."

"Good. What did Stacie have to say about it all?"

"That's one of the good parts of the day. When we were moving the boxes away from the water, the phone got disconnected. I haven't talked with her since this morning."

"Right. She's out of town."

"Yeah, she and Dan were planning to visit Niagara Falls this afternoon."

"As in Stacie and Dan *together* visit Niagara Falls?"

"Something like that."

"Interesting."

"Or not. Oh, before I forget, I met your cousin Matt."

"Matt?"

"Yeah, you know, dark hair, medium build, looks a lot like a younger version of you."

"I know who Matt is. Where did you run into him?"

"At work. He fixed the water problem."

"He has the apartment above work?"

"No, he's one of the management company's maintenance guys. And you'll never guess who owns the maintenance company."

"My father," he said, almost before she finished.

Score one Mike. "It's not Wheeler Properties. He has another company."

Now it was back in his court.

"I'm sure he has his reasons for a second management company. Money."

"Wait." She held up her hand like a stop sign. "There's more."

"I don't want to know more." He gripped the arms of the chair and leaned forward.

"No," she said. "You'll want to hear this."

"Candy."

She'd never heard him use quite that stern of a tone before. "Really."

"All right." He leaned back in the chair but didn't loosen his grip.

"Your father's other company is actively supporting the zoning change you talked about the other night."

"No surprise." He shrugged.

She couldn't understand his seeming lack of interest. His job was in jeopardy. And she thought he cared about his guys, wouldn't want them to be homeless. "From what I read, I think the company wants to buy up the whole block your vets' house is on."

Mike's jaw tightened. "He wouldn't," he said under his breath. "I don't believe it."

"I printed the articles, and there's a Web site, Vets Alive." She reached for her bag.

He released his grip on the chair arms and slumped back.

"Here they are." She held out a copy of the report she'd put together for Stacie and Dan.

He shook his head.

"Come on. And, I'll show you Web site on my computer."

"You don't get it." He fairly growled. "I don't care what he owns, what he does."

"But, your vets' house. I have an idea."

"So do I. Drop it."

She drew back the papers and set them on the couch beside her. Wow! Mara had said Mike and his father didn't get along. But the disgust and dislike on Mike's face went far beyond simply not getting along. Then, again, she couldn't imagine any parent knowingly doing what Mike's father seemed to be doing to him.

Mike stood as if to leave.

"Hey, new subject." She stuffed the papers back into her bag, wondering if she sounded as desperate to have him stay as she felt. She looked forward to spending her evenings with Mike, liked having a built in friend that she didn't have to dressed up for and go out and meet somewhere. "You never did tell me about the kisses in the dish. The ones you just replaced."

The corner of his mouth curled and he sat back down.

"So, who, what, where, when, and how good?" she asked.

The quirk turned into a full grin. "What is this, a news interview?"

"No. I'm just asking for the competition. We're supposed to report our scores."

"Scores?" His grin grew wider.

She sighed. "You know what I mean."

"I thought the candy did that. I have four; you have the three you just added."

"Yeah, but your four could be one four-candy kiss, which would put you close to winning." And her losing. She didn't like to lose. "Or they could be four one-candy kisses." The idea that he might be out kissing just any woman to up his score didn't sit any better with her. She gave her three kisses a guilty glance. It wasn't the same. She had genuine affection for Andre.

"Four one-candy." He looked like he was going to say more but didn't.

"And," she urged.

"It was the same woman."

So, he'd kissed a woman four times since Friday. She couldn't see any problem, except for her sight-unseen dislike for the woman, whoever she might be.

"They didn't improve," he explained. "The kisses," he added.

He seemed earnest, but he glint in his eyes made her wonder if he was teasing.

"If she liked the first one, shouldn't the others have gotten better?" he pressed.

"Um, yeah." She was still having trouble wrapping her mind around anyone not liking Mike's kiss.

"Help me figure out where I went wrong." He got up, moved her bag out of the way, and sat next to her. "We were at Jesse's."

She did a mental tally of all the women she and Jesse knew in common.

"No one you know," he said.

Her brothers *had* always said she shouldn't ever play poker because her expression was a direct line to her thoughts.

"Jesse has new upstairs neighbors," he continued.

He was kissing someone he'd just met—four times, nonetheless?

"Like I said, we were sitting on the futon like this, watching the game."

That was his date? Watching a baseball game with Jesse's new neighbor?

He slid his arm around her and gave her shoulder a little squeeze.

Warmth flowed from him to her at every point their bodies touched, making her uncomfortably aware of her wet, bedraggled state.

"It was the bottom of the ninth. The Sox were down three to one, bases loaded, and the batter had a three two count. Then, wham." He pulled her closer. "A home run. In her excitement about the Sox winning, Elise gave me a hug."

All right. Her name was Elise and she liked baseball. Candy's brothers were such sports freaks that, at a young age, she'd formed an absolute dislike of watching any sporting event. Maybe she should revisit that dislike if she and Mike were going to be friends. He might want to watch games here. Of course, he might want to watch games here with this Elise. She inched away from Mike.

"It seemed like a good opportunity."

"Opportunity?"

"You know. She sort of turned and I . . ." He bent his head toward Candy's, his eyes softly darkening.

Picturing Elise, no doubt. She was probably a tall willowy blond.

His lips touched hers, and she stopped thinking about Elise or anything else. When he lightened the pressure, Candy wrapped her arms around his neck and drew him back.

Meeeeow! The weight of Sheba catapulting into her lap made Candy jerk away.

"It wasn't me," he murmured.

"Hmmm?" Candy squirmed, trying to adjust to the clammy coldness that had replaced the cocooning warmth of Mike's embrace.

"That got better."

The kiss. He was talking about the kiss. It *had* gotten better. Better and better. She petted Sheba to calm her still-humming nerves. The feline rewarded Candy's attention by nipping her finger—hard.

"Ouch!" She pushed Sheba from her lap.

"You okay?" He took her hand and examined her finger.

The humming restarted full force.

"Chemistry," she blurted.

"What?"

She retrieved her hand. "You and Elise. Maybe there's no chemistry."

"No, she's really hot. You don't suppose." He halted. "That it's me?"

Not going by the kiss they just finished. "There's more to chemistry than just lust. How did you two get along? Did you have things in common to talk about?"

"Talk? The game. Nothing else really."

"There you go. Women want a little talk, a little friendship. A common bond fuels the chemistry."

"Like you and me."

"Yeah. Er." She swallowed hard. Where was he going?

"You didn't find anything wrong with my kiss?"

"Mmmm, no." She concentrated on pulling a loose thread from the rip in her skirt.

"Didn't think it was me. Elise and I just don't suit. Good to know. Thanks."

"Anytime." She went to work on the next string in the weave. Once she'd unraveled the next row in the fabric, she looked to find Mike watching her, a glint of humor in his eyes.

"So, how'd you rate our kiss? Three candies? Four?" he asked.

He knew he was making her uncomfortable. "Three," she shot back.

"Only three? Guess I need to find someone I get

along with as well as I do with you and keep practicing." He paused as if considering his prospects. "Unless you're game for a little practice. We were on a roll there before Sheba interrupted."

Heat crept up her neck and spread across her face in a full flush.

"Hey, I'm kidding."

His words extinguished the heat faster than ice water. Now he was irritating her with his teasing. Heck, she was irritating herself entertaining the thought of her and Mike as anything more than temporary roomies.

He slapped his knee. "Wish I had my camera phone. Your expression was priceless."

"That's me, priceless."

Mike tilted his head in question.

"Forget it."

"Hey." He took her hand in his. "You've got to let me know if my teasing bothers you. I don't want to do anything that might ruin our friendship."

"Me either." Except—she touched her lips with her other hand—push their relationship beyond friendship.

He squeezed her hand, and she resisted resting her head on his shoulder in response.

"Friends, then?" he asked.

"Friends," she agreed, disentangling her fingers from his.

"Do you have plans for tonight?" He looked pointedly at her candy dish.

"Nothing beyond going upstairs and changing out of

these wet clothes." Sheba meowed loudly and rubbed against her legs. "And feeding Sheba."

"A new DVD came in the mail today. Want to watch it with me? We could order a pizza."

Two hours alone with Mike watching a movie in companionable silence, the kisses in the candy dishes reminding her of their kiss on the couch. Nope. She wasn't up to it.

Her cell phone rang. Saved by the bell, or, rather, by the tinny mechanical version of "Fleur-de-Lis." Candy dug through her bag until she found the now-quiet phone. She flipped it open.

"Stacie," she said. This might be the one and only time she'd ever been glad for Stacie calling her at home. "I'd better call her back."

"How about the pizza and movie?"

"The pizza sounds good. But I'll have to pass on the movie. Who knows how long I'll be on the phone with Stacie or what she'll want me to do for her."

She pulled her wallet from her bag, and the report she'd put together for Mike fell on the couch.

"Here." She handed him her share of the pizza cost and picked up the papers to put them back in her bag. Her insides tightened. Why not? She placed the report on the coffee table.

He looked at it and frowned. "I'll let you know when the pizza gets here."

"Thanks." She headed to her room, glancing at the

reflection in the picture window on her way upstairs to see if Mike had picked up the report. He hadn't. If he'd talk with her, she was sure he would see she could help him. He was as frustrating as her brothers, just in different ways.

Once Candy had turned the bend in the stairs and could no longer see him, Mike picked up the papers and leafed through them. He whistled. She had come up with some pretty damning information. Like he'd told Candy, he didn't care to hear anything about his father, but the Alliance's attorney might.

He should tell her that, and that she should stay clear of his father, let the attorney handle it, rather than trying to turn it into a campaign crusade. He wasn't sure what Dan Burling's take on homeless veterans was, but he had a good idea that Stacie's was the same as Laura's—skeezy people best kept out of sight. Nope, he couldn't see Stacie jumping on the save-the-vet-housing bandwagon. She'd be more in line with Laura for gentrification.

He rolled up the pages and tapped them against his palm. It was a mystery to him how Candy could contemplate taking on Wheeler Properties, yet kowtow to Stacie. Come to think of it, she didn't have any trouble standing up to her brothers, or him. Maybe it was a woman thing. He shrugged, put the papers down, and hit the remote button to start the movie.

* * *

Candy dropped into the chair and turned the computer on. She might as well entertain herself while Stacie talked. As Windows loaded, she flipped her phone open, punched in the fast dial number for Stacie, and set her phone to speaker.

"Hello." Stacie's voice vied with the computer start-up music.

"Hi, it's me." Candy tapped her foot while the Instant Message buddy window opened. *Drat.* Mara wasn't on, nor was anyone else she knew.

"About time. I've been trying to reach you all day. What happened?"

"Oh, we had a little problem with a water leak from the apartment upstairs."

"The letters?" The pitch of Stacie's voice rose.

"Most of them were fine. We had to do one box over. They're all mailed. I made sure they got out myself." Candy opened her e-mail program. Junk mail and a reminder that her student loan payment was due.

"What about the equipment? The phone line. We're on a limited budget. We can't afford to replace stuff."

Like she'd planned on having a torrent of dirty water rain down on them for fun? "The equipment is fine." She crossed her fingers. "I don't know what's with the phones."

"They'd better be up and running tomorrow. Get the phone company over there if they aren't," Stacie commanded.

"I'm sure they will be," Candy assured her. "The property management company sent someone over to stop the leak and check everything out."

"You called them?"

"Yesss." Candy rubbed a rough spot on her thumbnail she'd split while chasing after Cleopatra. No need for Stacie to know she wasn't actually there when the problem started. "That's what they are supposed to do. Manage the property."

"Cute." Stacie's voice dripped sarcasm. "They'd better not tack on any charges for coming out."

"I'm sure they won't."

"You never know. Make a note to remind me to check the monthly charges."

"Got it." Candy opened Spider Solitaire.

"So, how's my Cleopatra? Did you two have a nice walk this morning?"

Stacie sounded as saccharine talking about her cat as she had when she was playing up to Dan and Mike.

"Oh, we had a lovely time." Candy clicked and moved a Queen of Hearts to the King of Hearts.

A knock sounded.

"Pizza's here." Mike lounged in the doorway holding a plate loaded with pizza.

"Who's there?" Stacie asked.

Like it was any of her business.

"It's Mike with my pizza. Hang on." She walked over and reached for the plate.

"What's that?" Stacie's voice boomed across the room.

Oops, Candy had forgotten the phone was on speaker.

"I think our connection is breaking up. Mike, you said? Did you ask him about introducing me to his father?"

Mike shot Candy a look that said if he were a lesser man he might have dumped the pizza on her. She grabbed the plate before he could.

"No, Stacie," she said in the direction of the phone as she raced over to switch the speaker off. "We talked about this before. I cannot get you an introduction to Paul Wheeler. I've never met the man." She smiled at Mike.

He pushed away from the doorjamb and stood ramrod straight.

"You don't have to get huffy about it," Stacie said.

Candy grimaced at the phone and mouthed "thank you" at Mike, willing him to leave.

"Tell Stacie I said 'Hey,' " he called before he walked away.

"What was that?" Stacie asked.

Candy glanced back at the door to make sure he was gone. "Mike said hi." She dropped her voice. "I wanted to make sure he was gone. You won't believe what I found out today about his father. We don't want Paul Wheeler as a supporter."

She briefly explained what she'd learned. "We don't want the campaign tied to him. The man's a—"

"Gentrification of the Mansion Place neighborhood," Stacie mused.

". . . sleaze," Candy finished.

"No, you're right. While cleaning up Albany is a good idea. It's a local, not a state issue."

What planet did Stacie live on? "Uh, I meant the veteran issue. The fact that Paul Wheeler's plan would put all those men out on the street.

"A bunch of homeless guys isn't going to help the gentrification."

"Stacie! Gentrification isn't the issue. It's—"

"Wait."

The thud of the phone being laid down was following by words she couldn't make out and a muffled noise. Kissing? Couldn't be. She shook her head to clear the thought.

"Dan's here," Stacey said breathlessly.

Ewww. Maybe it *was* kissing.

"We're going to dinner. I'll check back with you at headquarters tomorrow morning."

Click. Stacie was gone. Candy hadn't gotten any further with her than she had with Mike. When Stacie and Dan got back, she'd take it up with him. She couldn't just let it go. For the vets' sake. She bit into a slice of pizza. No, to be honest, for Mike's. Yuck, it was cold. She dropped the slice back onto the plate.

Mike was probably still watching his movie. She could go microwave her pizza and join him. Yeah, that's what she'd do. She turned off the computer, grabbed her pizza, and went downstairs.

Mike was stretched out on the couch—asleep. Candy ran her gaze the length of him, watching his chest rise and fall with his soft, even breathing and stopping at his face. His lips were parted slightly. She put a finger to her mouth remembering how those lips had felt on hers. A lock of hair fell across his forehead. She placed the plate of pizza on the coffee table and leaned over to push it back. The hum of the remote control on the couch beside him stopped her. It wasn't the remote. It was the phone. She pushed the off button.

Curiosity got the best of her. A quick check of the caller ID list showed a familiar number. Mara! Mike had been talking with Mara. Was that why she wasn't online? She was talking with Mike. Her gut twisted. *So what. Mara had called Mike. They were old friends.* She reached for the plate of pizza. There was her report rolled up, unread she was sure, into a tube. Candy took the pizza and stuck it the refrigerator. Suddenly she was very tired. But not too tired to give Mike another perusal on her way back to her room. She reached over and lifted the lock of hair from his forehead, reveling in its softness before pushing it back. The lines in his brow smoothed and his lips curved into a smile. Thinking of Mara?

She picked up her rolled report and thought about

dropping it in the wastebasket. Save Mike the effort. *No!* She'd put a lot of work into the report. Mike could trash it himself, if he wanted. She returned the roll to the table and left.

Chapter Eight

Mike massaged the crick in his neck he'd gotten from sleeping on the couch last night and looked around the Legal Aid waiting room. Its plain painted walls and serviceable furniture were a far cry from the beveled walnut-paneled walls and plush furnishings of the law firms where he'd spent far too many hours of his school vacations waiting for his father to close this deal or that.

Dear old Dad couldn't see any reason to sign him up for the break activities at the Y that his friends all went to, or to pay someone to watch him. He brought Mike to work and ignored him there like he did at home.

Mike tapped the rolled pages Candy had given him last night. His father knew he ran the Mansion Place houses. If he didn't know better, he might think his father was doing this on purpose to force him to come to work for him and take up the family mantle—or punish him because he'd refused to in the past. But he knew his father didn't care enough to exert the effort. As usual, pure greed had to be motivating him.

Candy had done a good job of uncovering some very interesting information about the proposed zoning change and who was behind it. He should have been nicer to her about it last night. It wasn't that he didn't appreciate her wanting to help, but any mention of his father got his hackles up and put him on the defensive. One good thing he'd learned from his father was to depend on himself and not look to anyone else for help.

"Mr. Wheeler," the receptionist said.

Speak of the devil. Mike glanced around. What would his father be doing *here*?

"Mr. Wheeler," she repeated. "You can go right in."

Mike sheepishly realized that she meant him. "Sorry." He stood and walked to the attorney's office.

There. Candy typed her concluding point of her PowerPoint presentation and hit the enter key on the computer. Things had been pretty slow with Stacie and Dan still out of town, so she'd taken the information she'd found online yesterday and put together a plan-of-action presentation on the vet housing situation to show to Stacie and Dan when they got back this afternoon.

The front door swooshed open and shut. She looked up. "Stacie, Dan. You're back early. How did the trip go?"

"Wonderful," Stacie gushed, batting her eyelashes at Dan.

"Could have been better," Dan said.

Stacie's smile faded and the batting stopped.

"Our numbers at the rallies and fundraisers weren't quite what I'd hoped for."

Relief spread across Stacie's face.

Candy bit her lip to keep from laughing. Stacie in love was more than a person should have to take.

"It looks like we have the endorsement of the Niagara Falls paper," Dan continued. "We're not sure about the Buffalo and Rochester papers."

Had Dan always talked in the royal *we*? She tried to remember.

"What's been going on here at home?" Stacie asked.

"Oh, let me fill you in." Candy waved them over to her desk. "Remember the other night on the phone when I was telling you about the veteran housing problem?"

Stacie looked at her blankly.

"Here, sit." Candy pointed at the two extra chairs she'd arranged to face her computer. She clicked the mouse and her presentation started.

"Stop," Stacie commanded as Candy clicked on the fourth information screen. "You mean Paul Wheeler is behind the zoning change?"

"Yes. Like I told you, he seems to be buying up certain properties through another property management company, not Wheeler Properties. I have more details in my written report." She patted the red folder on her desk. "I have a copy for you too, Dan."

She continued the presentation. "Paul Wheeler seems to be a silent partner in this second company. I think I told you that it owns this building?"

"Mmmmm."

Candy didn't have to turn around to know Stacie was pursing her lips and shaking her head

"I thought we were feeling Wheeler out as a contributor," Stacie said. "You were going to get his son, your friend—Mark was it?—to talk to him."

"Mike!"

"What?"

"Mike. My friend's name is Mike. And he runs the veterans' housing that would be eliminated by the zoning change. I told you that he doesn't talk with his father much. Probably not at all now."

"I'll bet you didn't even talk with Mike about his father."

Stacie had it right there. Going on their conversation last night, Mike not only didn't talk to his father, he didn't talk *about* him either.

"You have to look at the big picture," Stacie continued. "Paul Wheeler has a lot of clout in the state. This zoning change is just one example."

Candy turned in her chair to face Stacie. "He'd do that to his own son. You can't possibly still be thinking of courting Paul Wheeler as a supporter. Or haven't you been listening to anything I've said?"

"I have," Dan said. "Can you copy your presentation to a CD for me? And I'll take that copy of the report you put together to look at later."

Stacie's eyes widened at Dan's setback, and a thrill of triumph rippled through Candy.

"Sure," she answered.

Dan and Stacie stood as if to leave.

"When you're done, we have another little job for you," Stacie said.

Awk! Now Stacie was speaking in the royal *we*. Candy wondered if it was contagious.

"Dan's nephew is visiting."

They were going to ask her to babysit? Nope, not in the job description.

"He's transferring to RPI's engineering program, and Dan told him that if he came up early for orientation, he'd show him around." Stacie sidled over to Dan. "But the timing is bad. We're otherwise engaged for this afternoon *and* evening." She smiled up at Dan. "So we thought you could show Stevie around."

Dan shifted his weight to put a little space between him and Stacie. "Yes, this afternoon we have to work on my speech for the fund-raiser tonight, and then there's the dinner. I know it's short notice, but you'll like Steve. He's a good kid."

The word *kid* set off alarms in Candy's head. Dan wasn't *that* old. "So, Steve's a grad student?" she asked.

"No, a junior. He's just decided to pursue engineering and RPI is one of the best, so he transferred."

Babysitting. They wanted her to babysit.

"It's only for the afternoon, unless you're too busy here."

Candy looked at her near-empty desktop. She couldn't lie. "I'm pretty much caught up."

"Good. You can take Stacie's car and bring it back in the morning."

"*My* car?"

Dan nodded to Stacie. "We'll need mine for this evening."

"If you don't have plans for later, it would be great if you could have dinner with Steve too. If you have plans, you can drop Steve back at the hotel." He looked at her expectantly. "What do you say?"

"Yeah, I guess I can show him around."

"His train gets in at eleven. If you decide to do dinner, tell him I'll pay him back. That should do it." Dan started toward Stacie's office.

"Wait. What's he look like? How will I recognize him?"

Dan reached in his back pocket and pulled out his wallet. He flipped through several photos and took one out. "Here." He handed it to her. "Take this with you."

A gawky boy in a green graduation cap and gown smiled at her from the photo. Yep, she was babysitting. But only for the afternoon.

"You can leave your presentation CD and report on your desk for me," Dan said.

"Will do." Candy popped a CD into the computer drive and saved the presentation.

Stacie watched over her shoulder until Dan was out of earshot. "You don't have plans for tonight, do you?" she asked.

"I don't know. I haven't talked with Mike yet today." She was such a coward hiding behind Mike.

"You could always invite him to go along with you and Dan's nephew. Mike has a car, right? You could all use his."

"Nice try, Stacie. Mike's at work, with his car. I'll see how this afternoon goes and then decide about dinner. Now, if you'll give me the keys, I have just enough time to run home and change into some comfortable walking shoes before I have to pick Steve up at the Amtrak station."

Stacie fished her keys out of her purse. "You'll be careful?"

"I'll be careful with both your car and Dan's nephew."

Stacie gave her a quizzical look before turning heel to join Dan in her office.

"Hey," Mike greeted her as she came down the stairs.

"Hi. I thought I'd heard you come in. You home for the day?"

"No, even I have to be at work for at least half the workday."

She winced. "Sorry."

"That's okay. I'm on my way to check on some repairs at the other house and stopped to grab my cell phone. I forgot it this morning."

Her heat meter climbed a couple of degrees as he ran his gaze over the cami tunic and shorts she'd changed into.

"How about you?" he asked. "Playing hooky for the afternoon?"

"Not at all. I'm on special assignment."

Mike's gaze seemed to fixate on the spaghetti straps of her cami. "That so?"

"Yep. Dan wants me to show his nephew around town. He's going to be going to RPI."

"Grad student?" he asked, his eyes narrowing.

"No," she answered. "Dan said Steve was transferring here." She checked her watch. "I've got to get going. His train is supposed to arrive in about fifteen minutes."

"You're meeting a complete stranger at the train station?"

What was with all these questions? Mike was sure acting weird.

"Yeeeah. Dan gave me a photo to recognize him." She pulled the picture from her pocket and showed Mike.

His features softened as if he were relieved. "Looks harmless enough."

It was sweet of Mike to be concerned for her. Or could he be jealous? They weren't even dating. And she had enough older brothers already.

"See you later," she said.

"Yeah. And remind me then to apologize for last night."

"Sure thing." She bounded down the stairs. So he must have read her research after all.

"The Empire from New York and other points south arriving on track one," the PA system blared as the train station door slid open. Candy hurried through and crossed the lobby to the arrival/departure area. A few people sat on the vinyl couches. Midmorning was not a busy travel time.

She focused on the door to the track one stairway. A woman with two young children entered first, prompting a man to her right to rush across the room and embrace them all. Three middle-aged men in suits followed, then two younger men. She scrutinized their faces for any resemblance to the photo in her pocket and found none. The door closed behind them and the PA system announced that the train was now boarding.

Maybe he'd taken the elevator. She joined an elderly man making his way down the short hall to the elevator from the tracks. The door opened just as they reached the end of the hall. An equally elderly woman stepped out. The man took her travel case and offered her his arm and they strolled off in companionable chatter.

Candy stared at the now-closed elevator door. *Great! Now what*? She turned and followed the couple back to the arrival/departure area and scanned the room for new faces. One of the younger men was still there, talking on a cell phone. She pulled the photo from her pocket and scrutinized him. Tall, broad-shouldered, sandy blond hair. Not bad. But the only thing he had is common with the photo was his hair color. He looked up from the phone and smiled at her. She gave him a quick embarrassed smile and sat on the nearest couch to regroup.

"Fleur-de-Lis" rang from her bag: her cell phone. Dan must be calling her with Stevie's change of plans. She grabbed the phone and flipped it open. An unfamiliar number appeared on the screen.

"Hello," she said tentatively.

"Hi, this is Steve Burling. Uncle Dan gave me your number."

"Steve! I was looking for you at the train station. Did you miss your train?"

"No, I'm right here."

She scanned the room again and the hunky blond waved at her. That was little Stevie? Candy glanced at the photo, back at the man, then at the photo again. Couldn't be. There was *no* resemblance between the guy and the gawky boy in the picture.

A laugh came from her phone. “Bet my uncle gave you my high school senior picture. It’s a few years old.”

She looked up. Steve was halfway across the room. He stopped in front of her. The view was as good close up as from afar.

“Hi.” She waved the photo at him. “Just how old is this picture?”

“At least five years.” He laughed. “I should give Dan a newer one.”

Five years old. That would make Steve . . .

“I’m twenty-four,” he said.

“Pardon?”

“I’m twenty-four. You were doing the addition.”

“I was,” she admitted. “The photo. Dan said you were a transfer student.”

“And you thought I was barely out of high school.”

“Something like that.”

He smiled showing the faintest hint of a dimple. “I did three semesters at New Paltz, but had no idea what I wanted to be studying, so I took some time off. The first year, I bummed around. Then, I spent a couple of years building houses with Habitat for Humanity.”

He adjusted the strap of his duffel on his shoulder and Candy couldn’t help but noticing the way his polo shirt molded to his biceps. If building houses was what transformed gawky Stevie into buff Steve, the state regents ought to make house-building community service a mandatory part of all males’ higher education.

She dragged her gaze up to his face. “Ready to go?”

"Whenever you are." He touched her forearm. "Thanks for pinch-hitting for Dan."

"No problem. It got me out of the office on a beautiful afternoon and the use of my boss's car."

They walked across the station lobby and through the doors to the parking lot.

"It's the Z4 BMW in the second row." She pointed out Stacie's car. As they got closer, Candy pushed the remote to unlock the doors. Steve tossed his duffel in the backseat and they climbed in.

"Where to first?" she asked, switching on the air-conditioning.

"The hotel, so I can check in and drop off my stuff."

"You're not staying at Dan's?"

"No. Dan said he was going to stay in Albany tonight after the fund-raiser. I assume at his girlfriend's place. I didn't ask."

Candy concentrated on backing out of the parking space to fend off the nausea that waved over her.

"Do you know Stacie?" he asked.

"Do I ever. She's my boss."

"Great. Fill me in. Mom insisted I get as many details as possible. None of us have met her."

"You really want to know?"

"Sure." He smiled exposing his almost dimple again.

Candy shifted into first gear. A dimple, an almost perfect bod, and he liked to chitchat. What more could a girl ask for? She hit the gas and sped out of the parking lot.

The afternoon flew by. Candy couldn't remember the last time she'd relaxed and just had fun. Stretching her "workday" to include dinner had been no problem. Neither had hitting one of the local clubs afterward. She had to admit that this setup was a far cry from those her brothers arranged for her.

"So, do you want to come in for a while?" he asked as they turned into the hotel.

Candy clenched the steering wheel. Not exactly the smoothest invitation she'd ever received.

"For a drink or latte or something?"

She pulled into a parking space and turned the car off. He *was* sweet, but there was that something unnerving about his invitation, and she didn't know what.

"The offer is tempting, but I have work tomorrow."

"Right. And I'm sure Stacie will want you there bright and early." He unbuckled his seatbelt and turned to face her.

"You've got that."

For a moment he stared at her with a pensive look, as if weighing his thoughts. "I've got to head back home tomorrow right after orientation. My boss is expecting me at work. Any chance of your being my chauffeur back to the train station?"

"Maybe. I never know from day to day what Stacie may have in store for me."

He laughed, then grew serious. "I'd like to see you again—unless you're with someone."

Mike flashed in her head. She shook off the picture. "No, not really."

"Can I call when I come back up the first of the month?"

Candy wiped her hands on the gauze skirt she'd changed into before they went to dinner and clubbing. "You've got my number." Jeez, could she sound more cheesy? She studied her fingernails.

Steve reached over and touched her cheek to turn her face to him. He lowered his head and lightly brushed his lips to hers. "Yes, I do," he murmured before he pressed his lips to hers again.

Nice, she thought. *Firm, but soft. Not too aggressive or sloppy.*

Steve drew back a bit.

Shoot her now. She was judging the kiss rather than enjoying it. Candy made herself relax and concentrate.

Steve pulled her as close as her still-buckled seatbelt would allow and deepened his kiss.

Mmmmm. Very nice. Worth at least three candies. But something was lacking. Steve's kiss didn't make her want to melt into him like Mike's did. She pulled away as gently as she could.

Confusion marked Steve's face. He recovered with a grin. "Guess we should call it a night." He opened the door and eased out.

"Call me," she said.

He ducked his head back into the car. "You bet." He closed the door and strolled toward the hotel.

She watched until he disappeared inside, then started the car and left. Fun, intelligent, nice buns, and a good kisser. Steve was all that and probably more. What was wrong with her? She should be thrilled. She'd been complaining to Mike all summer about the quality of the few dates she'd had. Candy slammed on the breaks for a red light that appeared out of nowhere. Mike. That's what the problem was, and she had no idea what she was going to do about it.

Chapter Nine

"Hey."

"Ahhhhhhh!" Candy put her hand over her heart to stop her racing pulse. "What are you doing here?"

Mike laughed. "I live here, remember?"

"You know what I mean. What are you doing still up?"

"Waiting for you. How was your date?"

Great. Just what I need, another big brother looking out for me.

"Dan's nephew Steve is okay. We had a really good time." She walked over to the coffeetable, opened the drawer, took out three plain candy kisses, and dropped them in her candy dish. *Take that Elise and your one-candy kisses.*

Mike pursed his lips and furrowed his brow.

She'd seen that look every time she'd told one of

her brothers that the date he'd fixed her up with hadn't worked out. Interesting that Mike's reaction to her having had a good time was the same perturbed expression.

He cleared his throat. "How many?" He nodded at the candy dish.

"One," she answered holding his gaze.

"An almost perfect first kiss. Why not perfect? What was off?"

Candy started. *Steve wasn't you.* "I'm not sure," she lied.

"We should figure it out."

"Now?"

"Now."

Candy's heart started racing. "I don't know."

"Come on. Isn't that what our competition is about? Finding the perfect kiss?"

"Well, yes and no. We're supposed to be helping each other improve our relationships."

"And kissing is part of that, so should I stand up or do you want to sit?"

"We were in the car," she blurted.

Mike raised an eyebrow and sent her heart into overdrive. He patted the couch beside him. She sat.

"Show me," he said.

"I was driving." She stalled. We had just pulled into the hotel. He asked me if I wanted to come in for a drink or coffee."

Mike frowned. "And?"

"I said I had work tomorrow and we talked some more."

"The kiss," he prompted.

"Yeah, right." She took a deep breath. "He—"

"Show, don't tell."

She breathed deeply again and released the breath. Mike sat granite still. She reached up and touched his cheek, feeling the softness of his skin beneath the day's growth of whiskers. Her lips lightly brushed his. She drew back.

"That's it?" Mike whispered.

She answered by pulling Mike close and pressing his lips to his. When Mike responded, she pulled back and blinked until his face came back in focus. His eyes smoldered.

"I see. Like this?" He slipped his arms around her waist, brushed his lips against hers and pulled her close. Then, his mouth came down on hers soft and hard at the same time. She wrapped her arms around his neck as if her life depended on it and kissed him back. Seconds, minutes, hours—who knew—later, Mike softened the kiss and drew back. He smoothed an errant curl from her face and she shuddered at the tenderness.

"Do I have it down?" he asked in a husky voice.

And then some. She struggled to find her voice to answer. The rapid tattoo of his heart against her cheek that was pressed to his chest wasn't helping her in the search. He seemed as affected by the kiss as she was.

"Yes," she managed.

"The first or second."

The second. Both. Any.

"Candy?"

"I . . ." they both started at once.

"Go ahead," he said, his voice clearer now.

Embarrassment washed over Candy as she fully realized she was sitting on Mike's lap in the semidark, her face snuggled into the warm of the soft cotton T-shirt covering the hard planes of his chest. She scrambled off and sat a respectable distance away.

"No, you." She couldn't do it. These feelings were too new, and she was too uncertain of Mike. Let him go first.

"Are you going to see him again?"

"What?"

"Dan's nephew."

She shrugged. "I said he could call me when he gets back in town. Why?"

"No reason." A muscle worked in his jaw.

No reason! He was asking her about another man after *that* kiss. And he said no reason? This was where he was supposed to get into feelings. Like did he have any for her?

"Oh." She fiddled with the drawstring of her skirt. "Are you still seeing Elise?" She was as bad as him. She could just tell him what she was feeling. What was the worst that could happen? She could look like a fool and mess up a perfectly good friendship if she was reading him wrong. That's what.

"I haven't," he answered noncommittally.

She waited for him to say more. After a moment of dead silence, she remembered his phone call last night with Mara. "Have you heard from Mara lately?"

He looked at her strangely.

"You fell asleep. I mean I came down last night and you'd fallen asleep without turning the phone off. It was beeping." She couldn't be a pathetic as she sounded, could she?

"Oh yeah. She'd left a voicemail message."

"For me? You could have interrupted me with the message. I wasn't working that hard."

"No, it was for me."

He wasn't going to elaborate? Her stomach twisted. What did she expect? Declarations of undying love. She needed to keep things in perspective. It *was* just a kiss, part of their challenge.

"Well, it's late." She stretched, glancing sideways at Mike. He appeared lost in thought. Good. Better that he hadn't caught her little physical ploy for his attention. "I'd better get some sleep." She stood and walked toward the stairs.

"Candy?"

She turned back. "Yes?"

"Nothing. See you tomorrow."

Smooth, Wheeler. What were you thinking losing control like that? He hadn't been thinking. He'd been enjoying how perfectly she fit in his arms and how sweet her response had been. Candy's saying that Dan's nephew's first kiss had been almost perfect had cut him deeper than he wanted to admit. He had to grill her about seeing the guy again. And he couldn't stop there. He had to try to make her jealous. Candy was probably upstairs right now on the computer dissecting him with Mara.

He rubbed his temples. Time to put a stop to the kissing competition. He'd only gone along with it to help Candy lighten up and have some fun. What could a flirtation hurt? But that kiss was anything but light—at least for him. He had to get a grip. He knew he wasn't her type. A relationship with her would be as difficult. Candy seemed to want to get out of *Small*-bany, as they called it, as much as Mara had. *Yep, time to stop.* Before he fell too hard.

"Hey, what's up?" Candy asked, surprised to see that Mike hadn't left for work yet. "You're usually long gone by now."

"I owe you an apology."

Her heart sank. He was going to apologize for last night's kisses.

"For the other night."

Here it came. She steeled herself to not be embarrassed.

"You put a lot of work it that research you gave me about my father and the zoning change."

Reality penetrated her caffeine-deprived brain. He was apologizing about the other night, not last night.

"Earth to Candy."

"I'm here."

"Good. Apologizing isn't my forte. I couldn't manage it twice. I shouldn't have cut you off like I did. You need to understand that I try to avoid having anything to do with my father, even talking about him. I read through your information and gave it to the Legal Aid attorney I met with yesterday."

"You didn't throw it out?"

"No, why would you think that?"

"Maybe because you tossed it aside on the table and it was gone the next morning."

"Because I'd taken it with me."

So, he hadn't tossed it, and he was apologizing. She'd let the patronizing tone go this time.

"Apology accepted?"

"Apology accepted." She glanced outside. Rain ran down the window in sheets. "Any chance you could give me a lift?"

"I was going to ask you that. My car's in the shop. The starter went."

"Hmmmm?"

"You have Stacie's car."

"I forgot. I haven't had my coffee yet."

"We could stop at Starbucks first."

As if he had to entice her into spending time with him. "I always have time for Starbucks."

"Let's go then."

She dug the keys from her bag. It might feel weird

driving Mike around in Stacie's car like she'd driven Steve yesterday. "Here," she said. "You drive. Remember, I haven't had my coffee yet."

He grinned and opened the door for her. They dashed to the car.

"So," she asked as she climbed in, "you gave the stuff I found online to your attorney?"

He clicked his seat belt and started the car. "Yeah, I thought it would help."

"I gave it to Dan too."

Mike braked for the stop sign harder than necessary. "You didn't."

"Why not?"

"I'd rather you not get involved, get other people involved and make a circus of it."

"Hey. Dan seemed truly interested. I'm sure he's not going to do anything that would hurt you."

"It's not me who could be hurt."

Jeez, he was sensitive. "You know what I mean."

Mike circled the block a second time, looking for a parking space. A minivan pulled out from a spot right in front of the coffee shop. He pulled in. "I know what you mean." He shut the car off and turned to her, his face deadly serious. "But Dan is a politician. He needs backing to get elected. You don't know the clout my dear old dad has."

"Dan has a full war chest and the retiring governor's endorsement. He doesn't need your father. I don't think he'd take his support if it were offered." Although Stacie would in a New York minute. "Dan's genuine. He can't be bought."

Mike raised his hands in surrender. "I believe you believe that. But I'm asking you—and Dan—to stay out of the zoning fight. People who mess with my father and what he wants tend to get hurt."

"You included?" she dared.

"Me included. Now, let's drop this and go get coffee."

The opened their doors simultaneously and ran for the protection of the coffee ship awning.

"How can I help you?" the uniform-clad girl behind the counter asked.

Mike looked at Candy.

"I'll take a medium caramel latte and a chocolate chip muffin."

"A large regular for me," he said.

"Want me to grab a table? There's one in back. Or do you have to get right to work?"

"Grab the table."

"Okay. Here." She shoved the money for her coffee and muffin at him.

He shook his head. "My treat."

"Going all out with your apology, aren't you?" she teased.

"A man's gotta do what a man's gotta do. Now grab that table before someone else does."

Candy made her way through the crowded room,

breathing in the eye opening aromas of the patrons' various blends. She reached the table seconds ahead of a petite brunet in an Ann Taylor suit.

"Mind if I join you?" the woman asked.

"I'm with—"

"Jena!" Mike came up behind Candy.

Mike knew this tiny, perfectly proportioned woman with perfectly smooth, not a frizz in sight, to-die-for jet black hair? Probably natural. Candy touched her finger-combed mop that was way beyond its due date for a trim and highlight.

Mike placed Candy's latte and extra-generous muffin on the table in front of her. Jena had an espresso.

"You'll join us?" he asked Jena, not waiting for an answer. "Take this chair." He pulled out the chair across from Candy for her. "I'll grab another."

"Hi, I'm Jena O'Neil," she said, offering Candy her hand.

Candy half stood and shook her hand. "Candy Price."

"Oh, you're Mike's girlfriend who did the research he gave me."

Candy dropped her hand. "Friend," she corrected.

"Sorry." The woman sat and sipped her espresso.

Candy couldn't resist. "What made you think we're involved?" She took a bite of her muffin. Why did everyone seem to expect something between her and Mike? Her dad at the birthday party. Stacie. Mike's cousin. Now his attorney.

Jena tilted her head and looked at her for a moment.

Candy tried to swallow, but the muffin had gone dry in her mouth. What had prompted her to ask that? She didn't even know this woman. A quick gulp of latte helped the muffin go down before she choked.

"I don't know. Something in his expression when he talked about you." She shrugged.

He'd talked about her? Warmth that couldn't be totally attributed to the hot coffee flowed through her.

"He said that you might be starting Albany Law."

Candy held her breath. *Tell me he didn't say anything about that stupid bet with my brothers.*

Jena sipped her espresso.

Candy released the breath. "I'm keeping my options open, but for now, I'm good with Dan Burling's campaign."

"If you do end up at Albany Law, give me a call. We often hire research interns. Mike has the number."

"Whose number?" he asked slipping a chair between Candy and Jena.

"Jena's," Candy piped up.

Mike smiled over the top of his coffee cup.

She drank some more latte and tried to put things in perspective. At the beginning of the summer, she'd decided to find someone nice for Mike to help him get over Mara. Jena might be good for him. He seemed to like her. The latte suddenly turned bitter in her mouth. She swallowed. There *was* no perspective until she figured out what was going on with her about Mike.

Once she did, she needed to have a good long talk with him.

She lowered her empty cup to the table, crumpled her muffin plate and napkin, and stuffed them in the cup. "I'd better get going before Stacie sends out the state militia for me."

Jena looked totally confused.

"Her boss." Mike filled her in. "The Wicked Witch of the West incarnate."

"Stacie's not that bad."

Mike choked on his coffee. "Since when?" he asked once he'd regained his ability to breath.

"She was nice to you. She likes you." But everyone liked Mike—Stacie—Jena apparently, from the eyes she was making at him—her dad, her brothers.

"What's there not to like?" He grinned.

"Aside from your ego?" she asked. Personally she couldn't think of a thing, particularly after last night. Neither could Jena from what she could tell. Why had she made such a point of telling her she and Mike were just friends?

She crushed her trash filled cup, stood, and picked up the car keys from the table where Mike had set them. "Ready?"

Mike and Jena looked at her.

"For work," she said to Mike.

"I have a couple of things I'd like to go over with Jena."

So now he was putting work ahead of her. That she could understand. Or was he putting Jena ahead of her?

"I can catch the bus down to Madison."

"It's still pouring," she pointed out.

"I won't melt."

Did she catch a testy edge to his voice?

"I can drop you off. No problem," Jena answered.

No problem for you, maybe. Candy resisted giving the woman the evil eye. "Okay, then. I'll see you tonight."

"Right, sure," Mike said before turning back to Jena.

Candy pushed the coffee shop door open hard and stepped into another downpour. She slogged her way across the street to headquarters.

Chapter Ten

"There you are." Stacie pounced on Candy as she walked in, like a hawk on a hapless mouse.

Unfortunately, that analogy described their relationship all too well. Candy bit her tongue to stop herself from making an excuse.

"My keys." Stacie held her hand out.

Candy hesitated. "Does Dan need me to drive Steve back to the train station?"

"No, he's taking care of that." She wiggled her fingers.

Candy dropped the keys into her palm and walked to her desk. Stacie followed.

"Dan wants you to check out some more details on that veterans' *thing*. He's made some notes for you." Stacey nudged the red folder toward the center of the desk with a flick of her index finger.

Trouble in paradise? Stacie was obviously still in disagreement with Don over the issue.

"Sure thing." She smiled at Stacie, who turned her head and walked away.

Candy turned on her computer and hummed a popular song while she put her bag in the desk drawer and waited for the computer to boot. Finally, her e-mail program opened on screen. She deleted the usual twenty junk mails. She was about to delete another with the subject line *MELTDOWN!!!!!* when she realized it was from Mara.

You won't believe what I did. Can you IM me? I'm home. I couldn't show my face at work today.

Candy glanced around. No Stacie in sight. She double-clicked the IM messenger in the bottom toolbar.

Priceless: <I'm here—till the Wicked Witch returns.>
MaraNara: <Thank God.>
Priceless: <What happened?>
MaraNara: <Men are pigs!!>
Priceless: <Any particular reason why?>
MaraNara: <Luke is engaged.>
Priceless: <Say what?>
MaraNara: <The sleaze is engaged. And half of the people at work knew it.>
Priceless: <He is a pig.>

MaraNara: <No one told me. I'm still sooo embarrassed. I called into work sick today.>

Priceless: <What happened? How'd you find out?>

MaraNara: <Night before last, I went clubbing with some girlfriends and I saw him with another woman. I was fuming.>

Priceless: <Justifiable.>

MaraNara: <I didn't want to confront him there and make a scene.>

MaraNara: <Oops! Hit the enter key too soon. I was hoping he had a reasonable explanation.>

Priceless: <Like what?>

MaraNara: <She could have been a cousin in town for a visit or something.>

Priceless: <Fat chance.>

MaraNara: <Hey, I was really starting to like him.>

Priceless: <Sorry.>

MaraNara: <I talked my friends into going to a different club. I didn't want them to see him with *her.*>

A pop-up ad opened and blocked the Instant Message box, just as she heard the *click, click, click* of Stacie's heels on the floor behind her.

"What's that?" Stacie asked.

Candy tensed. She checked her computer screen for

any telltale sign of her conversation with Mara. "Just a pop-up," she answered.

"You'd better run that program the tech guy put on our computers. It's supposed to stop the ads. Want me to show you?"

Stacie reached for the mouse, but Candy got it first before she could close the ad window.

"I know how to run it. I have it at home." She inched the cursor away from the close button on the pop-up. "Did you have something for me?"

"More contribution letters. Before you check out those points for Dan, I need you to print out personalized thank-you notes."

Candy took the letters from Stacie and waited to hear the click, click, click fade out behind her. She closed the ad.

MaraNara: <Hey!!!! Anybody there?>
Priceless: <That was a close call.>
MaraNara: <???>
Priceless: <Stacie.>
MaraNara: <Say no more.>
MaraNara: <Where was I? Oh yeah. When I got home, I called him.>
Priceless: <What did he say?>
MaraNara: <I got his answering machine, and he had a new greeting saying "you've reached Luke and Jessica." I was so mad that I left him a mes-

sage I'd rather not repeat. Then, my computer modem was down, so I couldn't IM you.>

Priceless: <You should have called.>

MaraNara: <I did. Your cell. It didn't connect.>

Priceless: <Is that when you called Mike.>

MaraNara: <???>

Priceless: <He said you called the other night.>

MaraNara: <No, that was about my sister's wedding.>

Mara was calling Mike about her sister's wedding. What was that about?

Priceless: <??>

MaraNara: <I wanted to make sure I could stay there.>

Priceless: <Ah. How are the wedding plans going?>

MaraNara: <She's sticking with the orange blossom theme. Ghastly dresses. Mom loves it all. Need I say more?>

MaraNara: <Besides, we're talking about ME.>

Priceless: <☺ Go on.>

MaraNara: <Yesterday was my day off. A co-worker, who didn't know I was seeing Luke, called. She said Luke's fiancée had *finally* arrived in town and they were having a little welcome party for her. Did I want to come? I made an excuse.>

Priceless: <Big cyber hugs.>
MaraNara: <Then, I called again last night and you weren't home.>
Priceless: <I had a date. A real one not set up by Price, Price & Price, LLC.>
MaraNara: <Maybe I should have talked with Mike. He could always make me feel better. He's a good listener, even if he's not much of a talker.>

Candy bit her bottom lip. She had to ask.

Priceless: <Having second thoughts?>
MaraNara: <???>
Priceless: <About Mike.>

She certainly couldn't blame Mara if she was starting to see Mike's potential as more than a friend. Absence makes the heart grow fonder and all that.

MaraNara: <brb>

Candy opened her spreadsheet program and began entering the names and addresses for the letters Stacie wanted. The IM box popped up.

MaraNara: <OMG! He's here. I just buzzed him in. I want to tell him what I think in person. Gotta go. Bye.>

Mara hadn't answered her question. You know, it shouldn't matter. She'd certainly had the time and plenty of opportunity to pursue a love interest in Mike. Now, it was her turn—if that's what she wanted. So, what was with this guilty feeling?

The phone buzzed. Candy picked it up.

"How are those letters coming?" Stacie asked before she could even say hello.

"Almost done," Candy fibbed.

"Good. Leave them in laser tray and Dan can sign them when he gets back from the train station."

"Okay." Candy hung up the phone and finished entering the names and addresses. A couple clicks of the mouse later and the names and addresses were merged with the standard thank-you note text.

She looked up from her computer to see Dan coming through the front door.

"Hi," he said over the hum of the laser.

She waited for him to say something about his nephew. She'd had a good time yesterday, but last night with Mike was giving her second thoughts about seeing Steve again.

"Have you had a chance to check that information on the zoning change?" he asked.

She felt her face flush. "No, Stacie had me run some letters first. They're on the laser waiting for your signature."

And I had to get an update on my best friend's love life.

"I'll get right to it," she added, clicking open Internet Explorer.

"No rush. Is Stacie in her office?"

She nodded.

Dan picked up the letters and walked down the hall.

Except for his inexplicable attraction to Stacie, Dan was okay. She wouldn't mind staying on with him after the election—despite Stacie and being in Albany. A position on a governor's staff would look good on her resume. Or, maybe, she could stay on staff for two years and then get her law degree. With a law degree and experience on Dan's staff, she'd probably have no trouble moving on to Washington.

Either way, she'd have four years to be with Mike. Time enough to show him the opportunities he'd have outside of Albany. *If* she wanted to be with him. Candy grabbed a pen and drew a vertical line on her desk pad. One side, she wrote *Pros* and listed Mike's good qualities:

1. A hunk
2. To-die-for smile
3. Nice
4. Fun
5. Considerate
6. Smart
7. Great kisser
8. Gets along with Dad and bros

She stopped when she reached the bottom of the sheet. On the other side of the line she wrote *Cons:*

1. Mara might be interested in him
2. Closemouthed

3. Doesn't like help
4. Likes Albany

Then, she checked them off.

One: She could be imagining this one. Anyway, she and Mara had been friends a long time. She'd double-check with Mara before she let things get serious—if they were going to get serious.

Two: Maybe once Mike knew her better, she could get him to open up more.

Three: Ditto on the help. Or she could learn to live with him being reticent and him with her being helpful.

Number four made her pause. Mara hadn't been any more successful convincing him to move to Ashville than she had been with her—or Jesse. But maybe she hadn't taken the right approach. Candy was sure she could show him how much more opportunity he would have to help people, make a real difference, in somewhere like Washington. Then again, they might not still be together by the time she moved. What was she thinking? They weren't even together now. Nor would they ever be unless she made up her mind and talked with him. She Xed out the entire list—pros and cons.

"Did you get through to the Alliance director?"

Candy snapped the lead in her pencil. She hadn't heard Dan come back in the room.

"Not yet." I was too busy thinking about hooking up with his hunky property manager and had completely forgotten you wanted to visit the vet houses. "I'll try again."

"Let me or Stacie know when you have it set up. I'm free most of this week, except Friday afternoon. And be sure to leave that other information for me."

"Of course." Where was her head? She hadn't done any of the research Dan had asked her to do. She had to work something out with Mike, about Mike, or she'd have no mind *or* job left. "Want me to get those letters out in the mail for you?" she asked, nodding at the stack of envelopes Dan held.

"No, I'll drop them off on my way to city hall."

Once Dan was out the door, Candy ripped the sheet off her pad, crumpled it and tossed it in her wastebasket. Then, she got on the phone to the Alliance director and arranged for Dan to visit the vet houses the next afternoon.

At ten o'clock, Candy took the tuna steaks out of the oven where she'd been keeping them warm since she'd finished preparing them at eight. The sweet chili marinade had coagulated into a brownish mass that glued the Spanish onion rings and green beans to the steaks. She stabbed one with a fork and a chunk flew out of the pan to land on the floor. Sheba sauntered over to investigate.

So much for all the care she'd taken to perfectly sear the outside of the steaks to seal in the tuna's tenderness.

"Dumb, dumb, dumb," she said to the cat as she chopped the mess into smaller pieces to feed to the cat. Surprising Mike with one of his favorite dishes had seemed like such a good idea this afternoon. She hadn't even flinched when the grocery clerk had rung up a total for the dinner ingredients that came close to her weekly food budget. Who would have thought that Mike wouldn't come home after work. He always came home after work. She'd tried to recall him saying something, anything about having plans tonight and had come up blank. Of course, there wasn't any reason he should have told her about his plans. And he'd left his cell phone on the kitchen counter. She'd found it when she'd called him to see when he'd be home.

Candy scraped half of the fish into Sheba's dish and the other half into a plastic container for the cat to have tomorrow. She snapped a lid on the container and looked at the two dishes. So much for her romantic dinner. She was no closer to knowing Mike's feelings for her—or fully sorting out hers for him.

"Meow."

"Yeah, yeah." She placed the cat's dish on the floor and put the leftovers in the refrigerator. "Someone might as well enjoy my effort," she said to the purring cat as she flicked off the kitchen light.

Chapter Eleven

Dan opened the car door and Candy stepped out onto the sidewalk in front of a large Victorian-style mansion. Two plainly dressed men about her father's age stared at them from chairs on the wide porch.

"We're supposed to meet the director in the front lobby," she said.

Dan nodded and looked up the street. "Stacie called the newspaper. They said they would try to send a photographer."

"I know. She advised me to dress appropriately."

"That's my Stacie," he said with a smile.

Ewww! She checked her watch so she wouldn't have to gag. Dan in love might be as bad as Stacie in love. "Should we wait a minute? We're a little early."

"Let's go meet the guys on the porch," he answered. "That should give the photographer time to get here."

Candy contemplated the fifteen or so less-than-level concrete steps that led up the hill from the city side-walk to the house. If she'd known the visit would require mountain climbing, she would have worn something other than the purple wedge slingback san-dals she'd chosen to contrast with her natural linen dress and jacket.

"Good afternoon," Dan said as they reached the top stair. He extended his hand to the closest man. "Dan Burling. And this is my staffer Candy Price."

Candy preened. *Staffer* had such better ring to it than *gofer*.

The man introduced himself and Dan turned to the other. "I'm running for Governor."

The second man gave Candy an almost toothless smile and shook Dan's hand.

These must be some of Mike's "guys."

"You were here before when you were running for something else," the man said.

"State legislator."

"Didja win?"

"Yes, I did. I've served four terms in the state senate."

"I don't follow politics much. Think you'll win?"

"I'm doing my best to," Dan answered.

Candy heard a creaking sound to her left. The screen door opened and a familiar figure stepped out. Mike. She shouldn't have been surprised. She knew Mike's office was here too, but a part of her had been hoping she wouldn't see him here today.

He did his raised-eyebrow thing and she felt like someone who had just realized they'd spent the whole party with a piece of spinach between their front teeth.

"Dan," she interrupted. "You remember my friend Mike Wheeler."

Dan turned.

"He's the property manager here and for the other Alliance houses."

She watched the men shake hands. Mike must have court today. He was all dressed up in creased linen pants and a tailored cotton dress shirt that emphasized his broad shoulders. The only time he dressed in anything but jeans and a T-shirt for work was on days when he had to appear in court for a tenant dispute or eviction. She smiled. As if his tailored look was too much for him, Mike had rolled his sleeves to his elbows.

"Come on in." Mike motioned to her and Dan. "The photographer from the newspaper is already here."

Candy glanced from Mike to Dan. Had Dan heard the edge in Mike's voice when he mentioned the photographer? Hey, it wasn't her fault that Dan was interested in the vets and the zoning situation—at least not entirely. And Stacie had called the paper, not her. Being here was part of her job.

"The director had a scheduling conflict," Mike explained.

So Mike hadn't volunteered to show Dan around.

He'd been drafted. Great! That should put him in a good mood—not.

He reached for the door handle, but the door flew open first. A troll-like elderly man carrying a wooden case rushed past him.

"Ready for our game?" he asked Mike.

"Sorry George, not this morning."

George's face crumpled in disappointment. "You play chess?" he asked Candy and Dan.

"Candy does," Mike answered for her. "She's always up for a good competition."

Was he teasing her about the other night? Heat infused Candy at the remembrance of her and Mike's last "competition."

"Go ahead," Dan said.

Mike nodded. "You know you want to."

She did. It would give her the opportunity meet Mike's guys, maybe see why Mike seemed to like his job so much. And she loved chess. She'd been playing since she was five or six.

"Talk to you later," Mike said.

"Right." She turned to the wizened man. "I'm Candy Price."

"George O'Mally. We can set up over there." He pointed to a table at the far end of the porch.

"Have fun," Mike called over this shoulder as he and Dan disappeared inside.

Candy walked past the other two vets and took the seat across from George. He already had the chessboard out and was setting out his pieces. She started to line up hers.

"He likes you, you know."

"Pardon?" Candy held her queen suspended above the board.

George placed his last pawn. "Mike likes you."

Candy positioned her queen and went to work on her pawns. "We're friends. I rent from him."

"Naw." He waved away her explanation. "He likes you. I see it in his eyes when he talks about you."

Mike talked about her at work? A tingle ran up her spine. This was new. She'd never had a relationship where she and the guy were friends first and she didn't want to ruin a perfectly good friendship by pushing for more.

"Yep, he does," George said in response to her head shake. And you're prettier than the other one."

Candy finished setting up her pieces. The other one? What other one?

"The little dark-haired girl who moved away," George responded to her unasked questions.

"Mara?"

"That's the one. She's just a friend." His eyes narrowed. "Don't look at me like I'm touched in the head."

The other guys laughed. "The jury is still out on that one, George," one of them said.

"You *are* prettier." Impatience crept into his voice. "White goes first, you know."

Candy made her first move.

"That guy with Mike, he's your boss?" George asked as he studied the board or his counter move.

"Uh-huh. Dan Burling. He's running for Governor in the primary."

George captured her rook. "He gonna help us keep our house?"

"Dan's taken an interest in the situation."

"Good." George moved his bishop right into the path of her other rook. She studied the board to determine his strategy.

"Mike and the director think we can beat this ourselves. I've been around Albany politics a lot longer than either of them have. WW Two vet, you know. And I say it wouldn't hurt to have some outside help."

"That's what I think too," Candy agreed, glad to have some support.

"You know his father is behind this?"

She nodded, concentrating on her next move.

"Paul Wheeler is a real—" one of the other vets started.

"Watch it," George warned. "There's a lady present."

She blew her bangs out of her eyes. Like she'd never heard a curse word before. Did she have some sign floating over her head that only men could see saying cosset and protect from real life?

"Checkmate," George said.

Candy hadn't seen that coming.

"How about another one?" George asked.

She looked at the screen door and didn't see any sign

of Dan and Mike returning. "Sure." They reset the board.

"There's a meeting tomorrow," George said, interrupting her concentration.

"The Zoning Board?"

"Naw, Vets Alive. The Zoning Board meets on Wednesday nights."

She took his bishop. "The group that has the Web site."

"Yeah." He squinted at the board. "They're planning a strategy for the Zoning Board meeting." He moved a pawn. "Check."

Darn. Where was her concentration? She protected her king with a rook. "Do they have some more information that will help?" She scrutinized the board before she took her hand off her piece. "They should tell Mike, so he can have their attorney check it out."

"Don't know," George answered. "They mostly seem bent on taking some kind of action. They're really mad."

"The guys here and at the other houses?"

"We're mad, yeah. But I was talking about Vets Alive. They're a veterans' rights group. Want to come to the meeting?"

Candy knew better than to get involved with a group she hadn't checked out first. "No, I'll work with Dan and Mike."

George moved his bishop again. "Check." He smiled. "That Mike. He's something, isn't he? He's putting his all into helping us stay here."

Candy moved a pawn in front of her king. She couldn't disagree with that one. Mike certainly was something.

"I'd like to get some shots of the vets, maybe the guys I saw on the way in." An unfamiliar voice drifted from the house.

The screen door creaked open and Dan, Mike, and the photographer stepped out on to the porch.

"Mind if I take your picture?" the photographer asked the men in the chairs.

"Sure, why not?" they agreed.

When he'd finished, he walked over to Candy and George and introduced himself. "Can I take some shots of you and your game?" he asked.

George nodded as he completed his move.

Candy glanced at Dan. She didn't know how involved he wanted her to be.

"It's fine," he said.

"Are you a family member?" the photographer asked as he snapped away.

"No, I'm on Dan's staff," she answered.

The guy was really interrupting her concentration on the game. She glanced across the porch. Or was it because Mike was watching? She cleared her mind of the distractions.

"Check." She perused the board. Excitement bubbled up inside her. "Mate," she finished with grin.

Click, click. The photographer's camera filled the silence while George looked for a way out.

"You got me, good," George said. He turned to Mike. "I just might have to have your girl stop by every morning. Play her instead of you. Better competition."

Candy's smile froze at the words "your girl." She waited for Mike to correct George.

"You're stuck with me. Candy works mornings, and afternoons, and evenings half the time."

"Work is good," George said. He nodded at Dan. Then, his expression grew solemn. "But you have to leave some time for fun."

"We manage." Mike winked at her.

Candy felt her face warm at the memory of the last time they had "managed." But why was he letting George think they were a couple? Was he sensing the same change in their relationship she was? Or was he just humoring the old guy?

"Candy." Dan interrupted her thoughts. "We'd better get going.

She started gathering her chess pieces.

"You don't have to do that," George said. "I've got all day to pick up. But you have to promise you'll come back and play again."

"I will. I promise. Maybe this weekend."

"Nice meeting you," she said to the other men. "I'll see you at home." She smiled at Mike.

He tilted his head and gave her a questioning half-smile.

Hey, he was the one who let them all believe she was his girlfriend. Candy followed Dan down the concrete stairs, the satisfaction of knowing Mike's gaze was on her the whole way putting a bounce in her step. When she reached the sidewalk, she gave all four men a little wave before climbing in Dan's car.

"That one's a keeper," George said after the photographer had left.

"Huh?" Mike turned to him.

"I said Candy is a keeper."

"You've got that right."

"So what are you doing about it?"

Mike's thoughts went to Candy snuggled on his lap, all soft and warm. "I'm on it."

"Well, you'd better be, before someone else steals her away."

A gray emptiness fill the spot in his heart usually reserved for Candy. "You're absolutely right. Thanks."

"Any time," George said. "If you need any help . . ."

"I'll let you know. Now, I'd better get back to work." Mike pulled open the screen door and went inside. George was right. He and Candy had to sort out whatever was going on between them. He'd talk with her as soon as the zoning dispute was settled Wednesday night.

The morning sun had just made its way over the horizon when Mike heard the familiar thump of the morning paper hitting the porch. He flicked on the coffeemaker and went to grab the paper. He rolled it open as he walked back to the kitchen. Sitting at the table, he read over the front page while he waited for the coffee to finish. After pouring himself a cup, he leafed through the paper to the local section.

Candy's face leapt out at him. A shot of her winning the chess game ran along side a short article about Dan's visit. The caption identified her as being on Dan's staff and George as one of the house residents. Mike skimmed the article and returned to the picture. It didn't do her justice. While the photographer had caught her competitive excitement of her win, the picture didn't come close to capturing her true beauty or the essence of Candy that had drawn him—and now bound him—to her. What did he expect? News photos were rarely flattering to their subjects.

He heard the click of her sandals on the dining room floor. The kitchen door swung open. "Hey," he said, "you're news." He pointed to the paper.

She walked over and stood behind him, looking over his shoulder at the photo and article. The floral scent of her freshly washed hair embraced him, rendering him conscious only of her nearness.

"Ick. It's a horrible picture," she said turning away to get a cup of coffee.

Her scent trailed away with her. "Yeah," he agreed, fighting a sigh at its loss.

"Thanks! You didn't have to agree."

"What? You're a lot prettier than the photo."

She lifted her coffee cup to her lips and peered at him over the rim. A tinge of pink colored her cheeks.

"I meant it," he said.

The blush on her cheeks deepened until it almost matched the red highlights in her hair.

"Thanks," she mumbled into her coffee cup. She set it down and picked up the newspaper. "Hey," she said a minute later. This article isn't half bad."

"I thought it was decent," he agreed, "presented Dan in a good light, as concerned about veterans."

"Yeah, but the reporter could have mentioned something about the proposed zoning change."

"Nah, I think it's better as is. It keeps Dan out of the controversy."

"But pointing out the possibility that the veterans could all be evicted from their home, in the name of gentrification could gain you more support."

"Or more opposition," he countered. "Not everyone looks at George and the other guys as an asset to the neighborhood. Besides, I have confidence that our attorney will sway the Zoning Board to our side."

"I hope so." She finished off her coffee. "Now, speaking of George, why didn't you correct him yesterday when he called me your girl? You let him think we're together."

Mike shrugged. "That's what he wanted to hear. No harm in humoring him."

"I guess not."

Was that disappointment he'd heard in her voice? Because he didn't exactly tell George the truth? Or because she wanted a different answer? Sheba ambled across the room and inspected her food dish. Maybe the salmon would tell.

"Hey." He pointed at the cat. "She's been eating well lately. Dinner-date leftovers?"

Candy looked at him still a little blurry-eyed.

"The salmon."

"No, I cooked the other night when you weren't here."

"When I was at Jesse's watching the game?"

"Guess so."

"So it didn't turn out? The salmon."

"No, it turned out fine. I just made too much for one person."

She'd cooked for him? He warmed at the thought. Why hadn't she said something? He would have come home.

Candy got up, carried her coffee cup to the sink, and washed it out. "What do you know about the Vets Alive?" she asked over her shoulder, changing the subject.

He studied her rigid stance. They needed to talk—soon.

She placed the cup in the drainer. "Remember, I downloaded information from their Web site? George mentioned something about their having a meeting to-night to plan a strategy for the Zoning Board meeting tomorrow."

"Yeah, some of the guys have been going to Vets Alive meetings. The group's legit. It advocate for vet-erans' rights. But I don't think it's helping our cause.

The local group may be alienating more people than they're drawing to our side. It has a couple of loose cannons who aren't above using questionable—or even illegal—tactics to achieve their goals.

"Like?"

"All those tires slashed at the big car dealer up north?"

She nodded. "Price and I were talking about that."

"Price?"

"My brother, T. J. He's the oldest. I call him Price. Jase is Price Price."

Mike laughed. "You talk with your brothers? I thought they were your nemeses."

"No." She waved him off. "When I'm not stressed and they aren't telling me what to do or trying to set me up with their friends and clients, we get along fine."

"Yeah?"

"Yeah! Now back to the Vets Alive. George won't get himself in trouble with them, will he?"

"No, he's too smart for that."

"Good. He seems like a really nice man."

"Most of them are. They have disabilities that prevent them from living on their own or they're elderly, like George, and have no family or other place to go."

She nodded her understanding. "Well, I'd better get going. Stacie is giving me the privilege of attending a Chamber of Commerce breakfast meeting with her this morning and I don't want to be late."

"Ah, so, that's why you're up so early."

"Uh-huh. You know I'd have to have a good reason. See you later."

"Later." He leaned back in the chair and enjoyed the graceful sway of her hips as she walked out of the room. Like he'd told George, he and Candy needed to talk about their relationship and where it was going. Yep, right after the Zoning Board meeting.

Chapter Twelve

Candy stepped off the bus and maneuvered around the unsightly maze of dirt mounds that lined the street. Were they ever going to be finished laying the new waterlines? Seemed like the city had been working it on for years. She hurried toward city hall. Stacie had kept her late again writing and rewriting a press release, and now she was late for the Zoning Board meeting. As she turned the corner, she saw a crowd of people in front of city hall. A couple of police cruisers were parked at the curb.

"Candy," someone called to her.

She saw George standing with a group of men and walked over. "Hi. What's going on?"

"The meeting room is full." He waved at the crowd. "This is the overflow."

"Some turnout. Has the meeting started?"

"Don't think so. Mike's father hasn't arrived yet. Did you want to speak? You have to give your name to the officer on the steps. He said they're going to set up a television so we can see the proceedings out here."

"No, I'm just here to observe and lend Mike and you guys my support."

"Appreciate it. So are we still on for chess Sunday morning?"

"You bet."

A chauffeured luxury car pulled up and double parked by a local TV news van. A hum rippled through the crowd as a middle-aged man in an obviously custom-tailored suit stepped out of the car. Something about the way he moved seemed familiar to Candy, but she couldn't place him.

"Hey, it's Paul Wheeler," someone shouted.

So, that was Mike's father. She saw a resemblance in the planes of his face and his build.

A clump of mud sailed through the air and landed in front of him, followed by two more. He quickened his pace to a jog and ducked into the building.

Police officers raced from their cars into the crowd to apprehend the attackers.

"Oomph!" A man pushed Candy from behind in his haste to get out of the officers' way. Her bag slipped from her shoulder and her keys and lipstick flew out, landing in a nearby dirt pile. She bent to retrieve them. George gripped her elbow.

"Are you all right?" he asked.

She straightened. "Yes, someone bumped me and I dropped my house keys."

"Attention. Attention," a police officer shouted through a bullhorn.

Candy and George turned to see other officers hauling two men to the cruisers.

"Anyone who has not signed in to speak at the hearing, please disperse and go home," the officer with the bullhorn said. A roar of protest burst from the crowd. "I repeat, anyone who has not signed in to speak at the hearing disperse and go home."

Additional cruisers pulled up and officers went into the crowd telling people to leave. A few men sat down on the ground crossed legged, arms hugged to their chests when the officers approached.

"Let's go. This looks like it's getting ugly," George said.

Candy looked back at city hall and kicked her toe into the dirt. "I really wanted to be her for Mike."

"I know," George patted her shoulder.

"Move along," an officer said.

"Did you drive?" George asked. "I'll walk you to your car."

"No, I took the bus."

"We can walk to the stop together," he said.

"Sounds good."

"I had a good talk with Mike about you," George said.

"About me?" Candy wasn't sure she wanted to hear about it. Mike shouldn't have let George think they were involved.

"I told him that you were a keeper and that he'd better act quickly before someone else did."

"George, Mike and I are just friends. He's my landlord. We're not really involved."

"You should be," he said adamantly.

Candy laughed.

"I saw the way he looked at you when you were at the house—and the way you looked at him. And he talks about you all the time."

"Okay," Candy admitted. "I could like Mike as more than a friend. But don't you dare tell him. I'm going to talk with him about us soon."

"Atta girl! Make the first move. Us guys like that sometimes."

"I'll keep that in mind."

Diesel fumes announced an approaching bus. "Here's my bus," Candy said. "You'll be okay waiting here for yours?"

"Honey, I've been waiting for buses by myself since I was six. Don't worry about me, and don't forget our chess game on Sunday."

"I won't. See you then." Candy climbed aboard the bus and took a seat. Her stomach grumbled. She'd skipped dinner to get to the zoning meeting. A sign above the bus window advertised a new Mexican restaurant a couple of blocks from home. She had time to kill before the late news would have the results of the meeting. Chicken fajitas with nachos and salsa sounded good right now.

Candy heard the phone as she slid her key into the door lock. Maybe it was Mike with news about the hearing. She pushed the door open and dashed for the phone. It stopped just as she reached for the receiver. *Drat!* She went back and relocked the door. The phone rang again.

"Hello."

"What were you thinking?" Stacie screeched at her.

Candy held the receiver out away from her ear until Stacie's voice dimmed to a dull roar. "Chill, Stacie. What are you talking about?"

"The riot at city hall. It was on the ten o'clock news."

Stacie still wasn't making any sense. "There was no riot. I was there."

"I know. Why do you think I'm calling?"

"I have no idea."

"The news camera caught you attacking Paul Wheeler."

"What?"

"The clip showed those two men throwing rocks or something at him."

"Dirt. They threw clumps of dirt."

"Whatever. Then, the camera panned across the crowd to you picking up something to throw."

Panic constricted her windpipe. "Did the newscaster say that?" she squeaked out.

"No, but I know what I saw. People are going to recognize you from the article and photo in the newspaper and connect you with Dan. How could you? Didn't you think about what you could be doing to the campaign?"

The fajitas sat like lead in her stomach. "I wasn't doing anything to the campaign. I was picking up my keys. They fell out of my bag when someone bumped into me."

"Doesn't matter what you were doing. It's what it looked like you were doing. You know how important appearances are."

She did.

"What were you doing there anyway?" Stacie asked.

"I was supporting the vets. Showing my personal opposition to the zoning change." *And supporting Mike*, she added silently.

"If you're part of this campaign, there is no *personal.* Anything you do reflects on Dan."

But it *was* personal. Totally personal. Candy cared about Mike's guys and didn't want them to lose their housing—or Mike to lose his job. Now, it looked like she might lose hers.

"I was against Dan getting involved in the zoning controversy from the beginning." Stacie paused as if gathering steam to go on.

"I know, but—"

Stacie interrupted. "If you're going to be a liability to the campaign . . ." She let her rant trail off.

"I—" Candy started to defend herself.

Stacie talked right over her. "Dan and I will talk with you tomorrow," she said before she hung up.

Candy placed the receiver back on the hook. Her job was toast. She wished Stacie had just gotten it over with tonight, so she wouldn't have it hanging over her head all night long.

She walked into the living room and flicked the television on to see if the late news had the outcome of the Zoning Board meeting.

"Anne, we have a newsflash." The male newscaster interrupted his coworker's consumer report on gas grills.

Candy perched on the edge of the couch. Was the hearing outcome the flash?

"New York Senator Mark Shea has been pronounced dead of a massive coronary by doctors at Syracuse Medical Center. Shea was fifty-nine." The newscaster followed with a few biographical details. "Stayed tuned after the news for a look back on Shea's life and service to the people of New York. Now back to our regular broadcast."

Wow. Candy had met Shea at a fundraiser last month. He was the last person she'd expect to have a heart attack. Slim and obviously fit, he had extolled the virtues of running.

". . . excitement at city hall . . ." The newscaster's voice drew her attention back to the television. The screen showed Paul Wheeler dodging the dirt clods thrown at him as he made his way into City Hall. Then, the camera panned across the crowd and stopped at her picking up her keys.

Fury and despair battled inside her. It looked every bit as bad as Stacie had said. She couldn't even hope people wouldn't recognize her. The camera had caught her full face. Her hand went to her head. Did her hair really look that bad? *Like that really mattered*, she chided herself.

The newscaster continued, "The evening didn't get any better for the prominent local developer, as the Zoning Board voted down the zoning change he had come to testify for. Wheeler had no comment as he left the hearing steps ahead of his son Mike Wheeler of the Capital Region Housing Alliance, a major opponent of the change and the Alliance's attorney Jena O'Neil."

"We weren't surprised by the decision," Jena said to the on-the-scene reporter. "We had confidence that the city wouldn't turn its back on the needs of the men and women who served in our armed forces."

The reporter stuck the microphone in Mike's face. "Mr. Wheeler, how do you feel about winning over your father and his gentrification plans?"

Mike's mouth flattened into a thin line. "My sentiments are the same as Ms. O'Neil's. Now, if you'll excuse us, we want to go celebrate." He smiled into the camera and Candy's heart did a little flipflop.

She grabbed her cell phone from her bag and punched in Mike's cell number. She wanted to be among the first to congratulate him. The call went directly to his voicemail. He must still have the phone turned off from the meeting. "Hey! Way to go. Congratulations," she said after the beep.

She turned off her phone and the elation she'd felt for Mike fizzled. She should have been there with him. Could have been there if she had told Stacie she'd finish the press release in the morning and left when she'd wanted to. And now she'd be out celebrating with Mike and his attorney and not facing a future in the unemployment line.

Candy switched the television off and the house grew too quiet. She needed to talk with someone. Mara. She could talk with her about Mike *and* the job—or no job—situation. She speed dialed her, but got her voicemail too. What! Didn't anyone leave their phones on? She paced the room while she left a long detailed message. It was too late to call Dad, and her brothers would be no help. They'd see her imminent job loss as her being unable to stick with things and see them through.

She went upstairs and got ready for bed, but couldn't sleep. Every time she'd start to doze off, some extraneous noise would disturb her and keep her awake listening for sounds of Mike returning. She'd replay Stacie's phone call in her head and practice what she could say to Stacie and Dan to save her job. Then she'd list her other options. There was law school. Her acceptance letter had come last week. She could start in January. Mike's attorney had said over coffee that Legal Aid often had openings for research assistants. Her life didn't depend on her working on Dan's campaign. So why did it feel like it did?

Chapter Thirteen

Candy woke with a killer headache. She needed Excedrin—badly. There was none in the upstairs medicine cabinet. Using what little energy she had, she donned the power outfit she'd planned in the wee hours of the morning for her meeting with Stacie and Dan and applied her makeup before going downstairs in search of pain relief. A quick search of her bag didn't turn up any either. She couldn't face Stacie feeling like this. Maybe Mike had something in the kitchen.

As she opened the cupboard above the kitchen sink, she noticed there were no dishes in the drainer. Mike always ate breakfast. Must be he wasn't up yet. Or maybe he hadn't come home. His attorney Jena O'Neil talking to the reporter last night flashed in her mind. Her head throbbed harder. Candy closed her eyes and took a deep breath. Mike and his whereabouts would have to wait until later. Right now, she had to get down to headquarters and try to salvage her job.

When she opened her eyes, she spied a bottle of plain aspirin behind a box of Band-Aids. She washed two down with some of Mike's orange juice from the refrigerator.

Candy dragged herself down the bus steps and across the sidewalk to headquarters. At least her head has stopped throbbing. She pulled open the glass door and stepped in.

"You're late," Stacie greeted her.

Like it mattered when Stacie was just going to fire her anyway.

"Come on," Stacie said.

Candy stopped and looked at her boss. She was smiling. Come to think of it, her reprimand about being late had sounded almost friendly.

"We're celebrating." Stacie waved her over.

Dan lifted a cup of caramel latte. "We got you your favorite."

Now, she was really confused. "Celebrating?"

"Yes," they answered in unison.

Celebrating what? Her being fired? That would be crass, even for Stacie.

"Stacie has agreed to marry me." Dan's announcement was almost drowned out by Stacie's "We're going to Washington."

Candy took the coffee from Dan and sat down.

"The governor called Dan last night. He's appointing him to serve out Mark Shea's term in the Senate," Stacie gushed. "Dan's polls in the primary race are so good, the governor says he'll be a shoo-in to be elected for a full term in November."

Candy took a gulp of coffee. "What about the governor's race?"

"Since no one else in the party is as strong a candidate as Dan, the governor is going to run again."

It made sense. The governor would have another four years to groom someone to replace him and Dan's appointment practically guaranteed the Senate seat would stay in the party.

"Of course, Stacie will be coming with me." Dan put his arm around Stacie's waist and pulled her close. "So, we'll need someone else to head up the Albany campaign office."

Candy held her breath. Instead of firing her, was he going to put her in charge here?

"I've asked Phil Patterson to step in," Dan said. "He headed up Shea's Albany headquarters last election."

What was she thinking? Of course, he wasn't putting her in charge. She wished they would finish up all the happy celebration news and get on with firing her.

"Now, enough about my appointment. Show her the ring, honey. I know you want to."

Dan beamed, and Stacie giggled. Actually giggled. She held out her left hand to show Candy the marquise diamond.

"When?" she struggled out after another slug of coffee.

"Oh, you know me," Stacie said, "I don't like to fuss about things."

Candy set the coffee cup down and gripped it with both hands. Didn't like to fuss?

"We thought we'd have something simple up at the Gideon in Saratoga over Congress' holiday break in December."

Dan beamed at Stacie and nodded.

"How nice."

"Of course," Stacie continued, "there's still so much to do. Like my house. I'll need to sell it. Dan will keep his downstate and the camp on Lake George."

Here it comes, Candy thought. *The part where I'm off the campaign staff because of last night, but Stacie is going to generously let me stay on payroll as her assistant to clean her house out and get it ready to sell. Fat chance.*

"It will be so much easier for you," Stacie said. "You rent."

"Huh?" Candy stopped midsip. Was Stacie going to ask her to pack up and move out of Mike's house and into hers until it sold so the house wouldn't be vacant?

"No, I can't," Candy said.

Stacie's eyes widened.

Mike was so totally right. Stacie saw her as a doormat or less than a doormat, whatever that might be.

"You're not coming to Washington?" Stacie asked in disbelief. "I thought your father was fine now."

"He is," Candy stammered. "That is, he seems to be totally recovered from his heart attack." Why was Stacie bringing her father into this?

"I understand if you have family commitments," Dan said, "but this is a real opportunity."

"Washington? Opportunity?" She was babbling. "I thought you were going to fire me."

Dan shot her a questioning look.

"Because of last night at the Zoning Board meeting. The TV coverage."

"I may have been a little hasty in my judgment." Stacie actually had the grace to look a little chagrined.

"I assured Stacie that your 'indiscretion' won't have any impact on me," Dan said.

"I was picking up my keys. They fell out of my purse."

"No matter. I want you in my media corp." Dan hugged Stacie even closer and snuffled her hair.

Candy waited for Stacie to push him away and smoothe her messed coiffure. Instead she rested her head on his shoulder.

"Stacie will too busy being my wife and hostess."

And attempting to run the federal government.

"I know you're someone we can depend on. You did a good job here on the campaign."

Someone he could depend on? Media corps? Washington? The pieces finally fell into place. "You're asking me come to work for you in Washington."

"Yes," Stacie answered for Dan. "What did you think we were talking about?"

"You don't want to know." Wow! A real job with a senator in Washington away from Albany. And away from Mike and her family, and Mike and law school. Granted Washington had law schools too. "I don't know what to say."

"You don't have to decide on the spot," Dan said.

Stacie lifted her head and pursed her lips in typical Stacie fashion. Clearly, she couldn't see why Candy wasn't jumping at the offer.

Candy couldn't either. It was part of the vague dream she'd had since graduating grad school.

"It sounds great," she said with far less enthusiasm than she should be feeling. "I'll let you know tomorrow."

"You have my cell number?" Dan asked.

"Or you can call me," Stacie interjected.

Stacie's words squashed what little excitement Candy felt about the job offer like a bug smashing into a car windshield. She'd be working for Dan, but Stacie would be behind the scenes running Dan and everything else. It was almost enough to say *no thanks*, right now. Still the job was in Washington and once she got there and got settled, she could start looking around for something else.

"Yep, I have your number." *And Stacie's too, for that matter*. She gestured at the clutter. "Well, where do you want to start?"

"Oh." Stacie waved her question away. "We don't have to clean. We've got a service coming for that."

"So, you don't need me for anything?"

Stacie's face brightened. "I see. You made the trip down here thinking it was a regular workday. I guess we could have phoned you."

Could it be possible that Stacie was thinking, after the fact, about being considerate? Maybe Dan was having a good influence on her.

"To make it worth your while, you could stay here and supervise the cleanup," Stacie offered.

"Nooo!" She should have known better. This was Stacie.

"No," Dan echoed. "We'll stay." He turned to Candy. "I wanted you to come in, so I could make my offer in person. I didn't think of the inconvenience," he apologized with his best vote-getting smile.

"Yes, of course, we'd planned to stay. You can go ahead home, or whatever." Stacie beamed at Dan for approval.

Hey, maybe Dan was a good influence. The job in Washington might be all right, even if it involved contact with Stacie.

"I'll head off, then." Should she thank Dan for the

experience of working on the campaign? Or would that sound like cheesy groveling? He'd already offered her a job on his new staff. "Dan, I'll let you know tomorrow about the job. I really appreciate the offer." There, that was good; no groveling.

Stacie looked at her expectantly.

"And congratulations on your engagement."

"Thanks," Dan said, squeezing Stacie back against his side.

Oookay. Dan must know what he was getting into. He was a bright man.

"Talk to you tomorrow." Candy turned and left.

An unseasonably cool breeze hit her when she pushed open the glass door. Good weather for walking and thinking and she had no reason to get back home quickly. She needed to talk with someone. No, not someone. Talk with Mike. But he was at work. And Mara was at work. She really needed to figure out what was going on with her and Mike. No, she knew what was going on. She was falling in love with him. But she didn't know how strong his feelings for her were. He had feelings. She felt them in his kisses, in his friendship.

What was wrong with her? Dan was offering her what she'd wanted: a career job that would take her away from Albany. Or did she? She kicked a stone off the sidewalk, and it flew into the street. Was she really thinking of chucking it all for a man, a man who might or might not feel the same about her as she felt about him? Yes. No. She kicked another stone. There was also her acceptance to Albany Law School and a possible job with Legal Aid, or maybe she could stay on at Dan's Albany campaign office. And, her dad and Price, Price & Price, LLC, she added grudgingly. As big pains as her brothers were, she'd miss them if she moved away.

Candy stopped and reached in her bag for her cell phone. She flipped it open and punched in the Alliance's phone number. Maybe she could meet Mike for lunch.

"Housing Alliance. How may I direct your call?"

"Mike Wheeler, please."

"I'm sorry. Mike is out of the office until this afternoon. Do you want his voicemail?"

"Err." Candy shifted her weight from one foot to the other. "No, thanks. I'll try him later."

"All right. Bye."

"Bye." She snapped her phone shut and dropped it in her bag.

Dad, she thought as she trudged home. She could call her dad. He was a good listener. Or at least he was now that she didn't live in his house anymore. And, unlike her brothers he wasn't quick to dispense unwanted advice. Yeah, she could skip the Mike angst part and talk with him about the job offer and moving or not moving. It might help.

Candy shut the door behind her and took a moment to adjust to the strangeness of being home in the middle of the day. Home alone. She crossed the living room stairs and started up to her room.

Click. A door closed in hall behind her. She froze, then remembered that one of the new student tenants was moving in this week for the second session of summer school. A small chill ran down her spine. God, she was a real case. Here she was spooked by a chance meeting with a new housemate, while, at the same time, contemplating packing up and leaving everyone and everything she knew and moving four hundred miles away to Washington.

A scream rent the hall.

"Awk!" Candy turned, almost losing her footing on the stairs.

Mara looked out from under the towel she was using to dry her hair. "Candy. You nearly scared the life out of me. I didn't expect anyone to be here until later."

Candy stared at her friend. "What are you doing here?" Her racing pulse settled to a regular thump before apprehension began to build again. The bigger question was, what *was* Mara doing here, coming out of the hall to Mike's suite clad only in a towel?

"Didn't Mike tell you?"

Candy's heart sank as she watched Mara readjust the towel.

"Not that," Mara said.

Candy looked from Mara down the hall toward Mike's room.

"The other shower is broken. Mike said to use his.

Price, Price, & Price are sure right when they say you're easier to read than a learn-to-read picture book."

"What?"

"I'm not here with Mike."

"I didn't say that."

"Like I just said, you didn't have to. Too bad he's not as easy to read as you are. You'd know he's crazy about you."

"He is?"

Mara shook her head at her as if she were hopeless.

"So what are you doing here?" Candy gave her friend a big hug. "You don't know how glad I am to see you."

Mara hugged her back. "Could have fooled me a minute ago. If looks could kill."

"Sorry. Everything is so mixed up."

"I know. I listened to your voicemail message when I got off the plane. I thought it would be better to talk in person."

"You still haven't told me why you're here."

"You really have it bad, don't you? My sister's wedding. The orange blossom extravaganza. Mom's house is a zoo. You and Mike said I could stay here. Any of it coming back to you now?"

"Well, yeah. But I didn't expect you until the day after tomorrow."

"That's what Mike was supposed to tell you."

"Oh." The flood of relief was palpable. "So, the

orange blossom extravaganza. Is the dress really as bad as you said?"

"Worse." Mara grimaced. "Wait until I show you. Now let's go to your room before Mike comes home and sees me like this and you rip my head off."

Candy laughed and led her friend down the hall. It was so good to have Mara here.

She plopped on the bed while Mara pulled clothes from the suit case she'd left there earlier. "So, what's this about Mike being crazy about me?"

"As if you didn't know." Mara fastened the snap on her jeans and sat on the bed next to Candy.

"I didn't know," Candy protested. "I've been trying to get a read on his feelings for me—if he has any."

"Did you consider asking him?"

"I thought about it."

"Sometimes you're more like your brothers than you'd ever admit."

Candy picked at a ridge in her pinky fingernail. "What do you mean?"

"Safe choices," Mara answered. "Like, I went to Albany State because that's what I could afford. You chose Albany because it was away from home, but not too far from home. Even though all you talked about was leaving Albany for somewhere bigger after graduation, I knew you wouldn't just leave."

"Awk! You make me sound like such a wuss."

"You can be, but that's not what I'm talking about. If

you'd gotten a good job offer, and your dad hadn't had his heart attack, you would have gone. But you wouldn't leave simply for the sake of leaving. You're too close to your family. You *like* them.

She did, even though she complained about her brothers a lot. Their protectiveness had gotten her out of more than one scrape when she was a kid and worked well as a deterrent to guys she didn't want to go out with in high school. "What's wrong with liking my family?"

"Nothing. I wish I had a better relationship with mine. But, like I said, that's not the point."

"Then what is the point?" Candy slapped her hand on the bed.

"You're looking for the safe choice with Mike. You butted into his zoning problem—against my advice, I might add, sorry—and it helped. Who would have thought? So you're waiting for Mike to come to you and give you a safe choice. There are no safe choices in love. If you're looking for safe, take the job in Washington."

"Is that what you did?" Candy asked.

Mara released a harsh laugh. "No, I thought I could have it all. I never guessed Jesse would break up with me, although I should have seen it coming. Our relationship had run its course."

"Jesse broke up with you? I thought you broke up with him."

"I let you think that. My pride. Then, I tried to talk

you and Mike into moving down to Asheville. You know, bring a little home with me.

Candy's heart sank.

"Lose the stricken face. You know I tried to get Mike down here and that he and I are close friends. How else would I know he's crazy about you? He calls me and does nothing but talk about you."

Candy wanted to believe her. "There might be someone else," she said in a hushed voice.

"I don't think so," Mara retorted as if Candy had flung a major insult her way. "And, even if it is true, all the more reason to talk with him right away."

Candy finished destroying the fingernail she'd been working on earlier. "Mike's had plenty of opportunities to give me some inkling of how he feels."

"He probably thinks he has."

"How's that?"

"Ah, the kissing. I gather you've done a lot of that."

"That's just a silly game I started."

"And nothing more? All you got out of the kisses was the thrill of competition?"

She'd certainly gotten thrills, but they'd had nothing to do with competition. And Mike had been affected too. Their last kiss, where she'd ended up in his lap had said that loud and clear.

Candy squirmed on the bed. "So, why is it up to me to do the talking?"

"Because Mike's a man. Men don't talk."

"Too true."

As if on cue, they heard the door open and close downstairs.

"Go for it, girl." Mara pushed her off the bed and out into the hall. "I'll slip out the back. I ought to check in with Mom, anyway."

Mike was bent over the coffee table, his back to her.

"Hi," she said as she reached the last step.

He turned and she saw he was holding the nearly empty bag of almond candy kisses. Her stomach churned. His candy dish was full to overflowing.

"Hi, yourself." He poured the remaining candy into the dish. Several pieces tumbled out onto the table.

He must have had some celebration last night. She fought to suck in enough air to speak. "Congratulations on the Zoning Board decision."

"Thanks. We couldn't have done it without the information you found connecting my father to the zoning change. It helped to know who we were up against."

Mike's admission that her help made a difference was overshadowed by his use of "we." Did he mean him and Jena? Or him and the vets? She did have it bad, just like Mara had said.

"I looked for you," he said. "I thought you might come to the hearing."

He sounded disappointed.

"Obviously, you didn't catch the news last night."

"No, why?"

"I was on it. I got to city hall late, after the hearing room was full. I was one of the many people the police sent home after a couple guys flung mud at your father." Mike didn't need to know all of the gory details right now.

He crumpled the candy bag and tossed in the wastebasket.

"We need to talk," they said in unison.

"You first," he said.

She told him about Dan's appointment and his job offer.

"Great! It's want you wanted. I'm happy for you."

But he didn't sound happy.

"When will you be leaving?"

"I haven't taken the job. I told Dan that I'd let him know tomorrow. I have to consider my other options: law school, Legal Aid, maybe staying on at Dan's Albany campaign office. And Dad. I still have concerns about his health."

"But you're going to take it?"

She might as well get it over with. "That depends on you and those candies." She pointed at the table.

He studied the overflowing candy dish for a moment before cracking a slow grin.

Shoot me now and put me out of my misery. "I take it you've found the perfect kiss."

His grin grew wider. "I sure have. But I wasn't certain she agreed—until now. You'd consider passing up a job in Washington for me?"

"You're part of my decision."

His gaze drilled into hers.

"Okay, a big part," she admitted. "Does that make you happy?"

"Very."

"So which kiss was it?" she asked.

He groaned. "I thought the competition was over."

"Which one?" she demanded.

"Our first, last, all of them." He nodded at his candy dish. "I've just been biding my time to collect my prize."

"What makes you think you're the winner?"

Mike glanced from her candy dish to his to her face. "Oh, I am. Definitely."

He pulled her into his arms and lowered his lips to hers. This kiss was different than all the others. More possessive, yet sweeter.

All too soon, he stopped and nuzzled her ear. "We have the kissing down. Maybe we should go for the date that usually comes first. How about dinner and a movie?"

She turned her head to meet his lips with hers. "Later," she whispered, "later."

Made in the USA
Monee, IL
15 May 2022